ciations

y deepest and most
gratitude to:

Milton
th Burns
Rhead
y Gray
Urbaniak

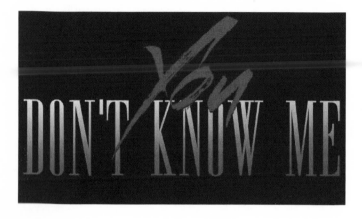

GEORGIA LE CARRE

ALSO BY GEORGIA

The Billionaire Banker Series

Owned
42 Days
Besotted
Seduce Me
Love's Sacrifice

Masquerade

Pretty Wicked (novella)

Disfigured Love

Hypnotized

Crystal Jake

Sexy Beast

Wounded Beast

Beautiful Beast

Dirty Aristocrat

You Don't Own Me 1 & 2

The Bad Boy Wants Me

Click on the link below to receive news of
my latest releases and exclusive content.

http://bit.ly/1oe9WdE

Appre

I wish to extend m
profound

Caryl
Elizabe
Nicol
Trac
Brittany

Author's Note

YOU DON'T KNOW ME

is a standalone Bad Boy Mafia Romance.
No cliffhanger.
Guaranteed HEA.

This version comes with a BONUS, brand
new additional epilogue for the Crystal
Jake series:
a sneak peak into a day in the life of Jake
Eden. Enjoy!

One

Noah Abramovich

"Boys will be boys, young men must sow
their wild oats,
and women must not expect miracles."
- Little Women, 1869

Tasha Evanoff! Blonde, blue eyes, plump mouth, and skin so white, it's almost blue, until summer comes, then, it turns wheat-gold.

What the fuck is *she* doing at the door of my office?

For a fraction of a second I actually think I must be dreaming. How can I not be? In that frozen instant I hear babushka's throaty old voice again.

'Listen carefully to me, Noah. The moment a newborn baby emerges into the harsh light of this world, it loses its magic. It adjusts and plays the game of life, but the powerful desire for the return of its magic never goes away. The urge

1

sits beyond the reach of memory and waits, because sometimes if a man is very, very lucky, his magic will cross paths with him again.'

Tasha Evanoff is my magic.

Not a living soul knows this, but I have secretly lusted after her for years. I forced my eyes not to follow her around her father's magnificent living rooms, or stare at her beautiful bikini-clad body lying on the sun lounger by the pool because I knew our worlds were never meant to collide.

Today she has wandered unbidden into mine.

Closing the door, she leans seductively against it, her sexual energy radiating across the room. She is dressed exactly the way I expect the daughter of an obscenely rich and corrupt man to dress. A flawlessly cut, knee-length white dress teamed with a soft-pink cardigan, and low heeled, round-toed, immaculately white pumps. Her only adornments are a subtle string of dusky white pearls grazing her throat, and velvet black clips holding her shining curtain of shoulder-length hair back from her face.

The intention behind her choice of attire is obviously not erotic. Virginal even, but the sexual tension coming from her fizzes between us like a bottle of shaken champagne. It puts my nerves on high alert.

I stand.

'Hello, Noah,' she drawls. Her father is a Russian bastard, but her mother comes from British blue-blood stock and her accent is pure upper class.

'Why are you here, Tasha?' I ask. My body is taut and hormones are buzzing all over the place, but my voice comes out flat and devoid of all expression.

'Surely, you're going to allow me to sit first,' she says with a hint of irritation.

'Of course.' I wave towards the chairs opposite my desk.

She walks towards the chair on the left, slips into it, and puts her knees firmly together. Her eyes are beautiful blue stars, the pupils, dark pits of nothing.

Would you like a drink?' I offer politely.

'Thank you, no,' she refuses, then she thinks better of it. 'Actually, yes, I will have one.'

'What can I get you?'

Her gaze flickers over me. 'Um … cognac if you have it.' And after a slight pause, 'Make it a double.'

I walk to the bar and feel her eyes burning into my back as I automatically pull glasses from the cabinet. My mind is churning. I grab the cognac bottle and uncap it. One thing is for sure: She didn't just happen to be in the neighborhood.

I tilt the bottle and pour out a generous measure.

I try to think why she is here and I cannot imagine any reason she could possibly have for coming to my office at this time of the night. I wipe the frown from my forehead and turn around. Casually, I walk up to her and hold out the drink.

She lets her fingers brush mine as she takes it. Of course, they are as befits the pampered daughter of a dangerous man, silky soft.

'Aren't you having one?' she asks, one eyebrow arched.

'No.' My voice sounds thick and strange.

'Oh,' she exclaims, gazing up at me.

It's like looking down at an angel or an apparition. It has a hypnotizing almost paralyzing effect on me, probably because I've never been this close to her before. I struggle with the crazy urge to grab her and devour her sulky mouth.

Fuck! I need to put something between us. I walk around my desk and sit down. Silently, I watch her drain the glass. The way her white throat moves as she swallows, the movement so erotic my cock stirs. She clasps the empty glass loosely in her lap and looks at it. The silence stretches between us.

Odd. Tight. Strained.

But I hold my tongue. Let her break it.

Finally, she looks up. 'I'm ... getting ... married in six months,' she says quietly.

I already knew that little fact, Tasha. You're marrying the good-for-nothing son of a psychopathic billionaire. It's a marriage brokered in hell by her fat fuck father, a thoroughly ugly and detestable man. If he knew she was here it wouldn't be a pretty sight. Blood on the floor would be the least of it.

I say nothing and she fixes me with those unnerving eyes of hers.

'Well, anyway, I thought that before I settle down I'd like to try life a little.'

'Oh yeah?' I can't fucking believe she's going where I think she's going.

'Yeah. I want you to have sex with me tonight,' she says very quickly into the tense air.

Two

Noah Abramovich

My entire body reacts to her words. My heart hammers in my chest and blood races so fast into my cock it hurts, but years of training keeps my face poker straight. Until today she has never even so much as looked in my direction and now she wants me to fuck her. Something's not right. I steeple my hands on the table.

'You might need to explain yourself a little bit more.'

She gives a one-shoulder shrug, a careless, elegant, infuriating movement. 'What's to explain? I want us to ... fuck.' The Princess had to struggle to get that last word out.

'Why?'

'Because ... because I want to be ... taken by someone like you.'

Like me. Now, I get it. The spoilt, bored rich girl is going to become the

spoilt bored wife of a spineless fool, but before she submits to that endless boredom she wants to experience something dirty with someone from the wrong end of town.

The Princess wants to be a slut for one night. And the person she has chosen is me. I lean back in my chair and let my eyes roll all over her. Well, well, well. All that untouchable beauty just laid out for me to soil and dishonor.

'What makes you think I want one night with you?'

Her smooth brow crinkles. 'Don't all men want a no strings, dirty night with a perfect stranger?'

I stare at her. This is what happens when you shelter your daughter to death.

She mistakes my silence for reluctance. As if any man in his right man would refuse her. Swallowing hard she straightens her spine as steely determination sparkles in her eyes. She has, after all, come from her father's loins.

'There will be no consequences to you. No one will ever know.
After tonight we will probably never meet

again, and even if we do it will be as if this night never happened.'

'Where does your father think you are now?'

She licks those lips that I want to bite. 'In my bed. Asleep.'

As if my lustful thought has transferred to her, her white teeth sink into her bottom lip. I inhale sharply. Pure lust is a powerful, bewitching thing. I have always detested weak people whose only excuse for doing things they shouldn't is:

It was the moment. I simply couldn't help myself.

In that instant I get what they are talking about. Every cell in my body is screaming at me not to take the poisoned chalice, but as if she has cast a spell on me, I stand up, walk around the desk like a zombie, and hold out my hand.

She wants dirty sex.

I know *all* about that.

Sure I'll give her a night so dirty her toes will curl. I'll make it so unforgettable that in years to come while her husband's half-flaccid dick labors inside her, she will close her eyes and remember my cock thrusting inside her.

A glimmer of a smile appears on her lips. She puts her hand in mine, I tug at it, and she allows herself to tumble against my body. Her body is softly curving and immediately molds itself into the hardness of mine. Her perfume rises up and fills my nostrils. I breathe it in. It's been a long time, in fact, I can't remember the last time a woman could disarm me in this way. *But she only wants dirty sex with you. She is yours only tonight.*

'Are you wet?' I ask, my voice harsh.

She shakes her head, her eyes huge.

My eyebrows rise. 'You sure about that?'

'Yes.' Defiant.

Without warning I grab her round ass and stick my other hand under her chaste dress. She struggles, but I tighten my hold, making her efforts puny and useless. Her eyes flash as my hand slips beneath her panties and touches her bare pussy. I plunge two fingers into her cunt. She gasps and goes rigid.

'Then ...' I extract my fingers from inside her. 'What the fuck is this?' I ask softly as I wipe my fingers on her downy cheek.

Her amazing eyes flicker.

I bend my head and lick her cheek where I smeared her slick juices. She tastes like musky honey. Unforgettable. I already know I'll miss her taste when she leaves in the early morning hours. Deeply inhaling the scent of her I force my tongue into her mouth. At first she doesn't do anything, and then she starts to suck it. *Fuck it this woman drives me crazy*. I withdraw my tongue and look at her. My cock is straining against the zipper of my jeans.

'You're never going to have another night like this so no more coy games and no more lies tonight, understood?'

She nods silently.

'Are you wet?'

'Yes.'

'How wet?'

'Dripping,' she says hoarsely.

I smile faintly. 'Will you do anything I ask tonight?'

'Yes. Anything.'

Three

Tasha Evanoff

https://www.youtube.com/watch?v=M6
G1oQgJm1o
Wet

He steps away from me suddenly and I feel as if someone just replaced my kneecaps with Rowntree jelly sweets. He walks to his desk, leans his slim hips against the edge and crosses his arms over his chest.

Under the overhead light his black hair glints, but his eyes are shadowy and hooded, impossible to tell the expression in them, but I feel their sultry gaze unhurriedly travel over my body. Raw, feral animal magnetism rolls out of him in waves that hit me and bring a rush of heat to my belly. I become as vulnerable and exposed as if I am naked.

'Take your panties off.' His voice is pleasant, but throbs with heat.

My breath speeds. Surely he doesn't mean for us to do it here. Maybe he imagines he can degrade me as if I was some sort of prostitute he has hired for the night just because I offered my body. I won't have it. My spine straightens.

'Are we going to ... um ... do it here?'

'No.'

'Then why?'

He remains motionless. 'Because I want you to.'

No one has ever spoken to me with such fearless disrespect, uncaring if they might hurt my father's feelings. A thrill of excitement goes through me. The air crackles with sexual tension as I slowly, deliberately, slip my hands under the hem of my dress and drag my underwear down my legs. I let them fall to the ground and step out of them.

'Bring them to me,' he barks.

I bend down, pick up the lacy scrap, and dangling them on one finger walk up to him. He puts his hand out, the palm outstretched and I drop the lace into it.

He smiles, his eyes smooth like wet marble, the skin at the outer corners

13

crinkling. He blinks—he has eyelashes a girl would kill for—and my breath catches in my throat. I feel as if he's cast a magic spell on me. I can hardly think. The air seems thick and every breath I suck in is difficult and noisy.

The intoxication is so complete I don't see what he does with my underwear. One moment he is holding it and the next his empty hand is touching my lip. The skin on his thumb is rough.

'Tasha Evanoff,' he breathes softly.

My lips part.

His hand gently releases my clips. 'You won't need any of these where we are going.' The clips fall noiselessly to the carpet.

He tunnels his hand into my hair, fists it at my nape, and pulls so the curve of my throat is exposed to him. My belly tightens with the look of pure lust that comes into his eyes. He pulls me toward him with a fierceness that startles me. I fall onto his hard body and stare mesmerized up into the scorching depths of his black eyes. Feverish excitement races through me. Between my legs I glow and pulse. Lord, I've *never* wanted a man like this.

'Fuck, there is not enough of the night left for what I want to do to you,' he says suddenly, and in one smooth movement straightens, pulling me upright with him.

He phones someone called Viktor and tells him to pick him up at the backdoor. Then we go out through the back of his nightclub, my body stiff with tension. Sometimes his hand arrives on the small of my back to guide me in the right direction. He puts out a big hand and pushes open the double doors of the kitchen. Every man in that kitchen gapes at the sight of Noah and me. I guess he doesn't make a habit of going out through the back with his women. Outside it is chilly and I shiver.

'Cold?' he asks, looking down at me

'A little.'

A car is waiting, and the driver, presumably Viktor, is standing beside the open back door. His eyes widen slightly at the sight of me before he blanks them of all expression. I wonder if he has recognized me, but it is extremely unlikely. My father keeps me well out of his world. I thank him and get in while

Noah walks around to the other side and slides in beside me.

'Turn the heating up,' he tells the driver.

'Thank you,' I whisper.

He turns to look at me, his strong cheekbones catching the light from the streetlamps and the look in his eyes makes me lick my lips.

Four

Noah Abramovich

My eyes drop to her plump lower lip, to the way it glistens enticingly in the darkness. It fucks me up some. I tell myself, stay cool, but excitement is like an electric current in my blood, zipping through my veins. Fuck, I have never known such blind urgency.

I want to grab her and take her there and then. And damn if it won't feel good.

I clench my jaw and turn away. There's a jeering voice in my head. *Stay hard, Noah. It's just one fucking night. Don't get your knickers in a twist.* I stare out of the window as the familiar streets rush by. I have done this journey thousands of times, but there is something surreal about this night.

Its name is Tasha Evanoff. Her perfume. Her presence, the creamy whiteness of her soft skin, the innocence in her wide eyes. I am a monster. I can bring her nothing but pain and ruin. Even touching the Princess would be defiling her, and yet, I cannot stop myself.

She is my one weakness. The beloved daughter of the Mafia king is about to become my worst fucking nightmare. I cannot resist her call. I've played this out in my fantasies too many times. Just one night. It's just lust. When the sun comes up it will be over. I won't chase her. I won't ruin her life. Just one night.

As the car eats up the miles, every cell in my body heats up, becomes super alert. Like a wolf I can hear her heartbeat, feel the heat coming from her body.

The car comes to a smooth stop. *Here we are Noah, you and your fantasy woman.* I get out and Viktor rushes to open the door for her. She gets out and looks at me. I thank Viktor and he drives off.

Cold wind drags at her clothes and hair. She hugs herself.

'My place,' I say softly.

'It's nice,' she replies without sarcasm. It's just a six-bedroom Regency town house with high ceilings and tall windows. But modest. Certainly nothing compared to the gold and marble palace she lives in. Russians with money are like Arabs. Flashy. They invest in ostentation.

'Sure you want to do this?'

She reaches out a hand and, with her thumb and forefinger, picks something from my right cheek. Staring at me she holds it in front of my lips. It is an old Russian superstition: if an eyelash falls out you will receive a gift. My chest feels tight. My mother used to do this to me. Take the eyelash and let me blow it away while making a wish.

I blow. Strands of her blonde hair lift away from her neck.

She blinks. 'Did you make a wish?'

I nod. How surprised she would be if she knew what I wished for. How surprised I am at my fucking wish. None of the wishes I made when my mother held the eyelash ever came true. There is absolutely no way this one is going to either.

We walk up the steps and I put the key in my door. I close the door and watch her look at her surroundings.

'Want a drink?' I offer.

'If you'll have one too?'

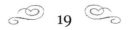

I walk to the first reception room and switch on the light.

She laughs, a breathless sound. 'Wow, it's beautiful.'

I look at the decor as if for the first time. Through her eyes. I never notice it anymore. I follow her eyes as she takes in the pale ice cream colors on the walls, the charcoal grey floor, and the dark silk curtains. There are red velvet cushions on the white fainting couch. She moves deeper into the room to stand on the soft-lilac shag carpet.

'I never would have imagined you lived in a house like this.'

I shrug casually. This is my house, but it is not a home. I don't really live here. In fact, I hardly come. Often I crash in the apartment above my restaurant. 'I didn't actually decorate it. I hired someone.'

'Of course, I knew that, but you approved her design.'

'When I buy a dog I tend not to bark myself.'

She laughs again, but this time it is for real. A lovely sound. It's the way I thought she might sound. Rich, sexy, and exhilarating. 'I just expected more black leather and chrome somehow.' She stops and shrugs. 'I mean being *bratva* and all.'

'I'm not in the brotherhood anymore,' I say quietly.

She cocks an eyebrow. 'Oh, since when?'

'Years,' I say simply.

'So you just walked away from it?' she asks curiously.

'You never walk away from it. It walks beside you.'

'What does that mean?'

'Your sins, every one of them, they never leave you, no matter how far you run, or how long you live.'

She stares at me.

'But you didn't come here to talk about my sins.'

She doesn't say anything so I move to the drinks cabinet and pour us each a large measure of cognac. She takes hers from my hand and raises it.

'To tonight,' she says.

'Tonight,' I reply and we both drink.

To my surprise she knocks it back as fast as me. She is so beautiful she makes my cock weep. I want to tear the clothes off her, but she will need to go home in them before the sun rises again. The thought doesn't sit well. I already dread having to let her go tomorrow. Once I possess her ...

She reaches out a hand and unbuttons my shirt, exposing my chest. Her pale finger, the nail painted pearly pink, traces the tattoo of a roaring tiger on my chest.

'*Oskal* (bared teeth) You were a thief,' she breathes.

I don't say anything. My tattoos tell their own tale of bloodshed, violence, and the unspoken moral code of my past. My time of treading a fine line between life and death. The punishment for getting a tattoo you have not earned is severe so they work as my CV, and being the daughter of a mafia king she can read each letter and design like a language.

She undoes the rest of the buttons on my shirt, pulls the shirttails out, and slips it off me. I watch her eyes hungrily take in the width of me, before her eyes alight on the tattoo of an epaulette inked onto my right shoulder.

'High ranking,' she whispers.

She rises to her tiptoes and kisses me right on the skull in the middle of the epaulette. It is a gesture of approval. She

knows it signifies that I am not, or will ever be a slave to anyone.

I stand as still as a statue when she touches the rose. So many memories come crowding back. No other woman has touched it quite the same way. It is Delilah holding Samson's hair.

'You spent your eighteenth birthday in prison,' she notes. Her voice grave.

Then her finger delicately trails the blade of a dagger. 'You have taken life.' She touches the drops of blood as she counts aloud the lives I have taken. 'One, two, three, four ...' There are more drops, but she doesn't go on. She looks up at me, our gazes touch, and she exhales a long breath. It sounds like regret or pain.

She walks around the back and looks at the massive tattoo of the Madonna and Child surrounded by saints and angels. In the background a cathedral. It is a thieves' talisman. *I know I am a sinner but protect me, guide me, bring me luck.*

'So ... you were a thief from an early age,' she deciphers. I feel her breath warm on my back.

'Fifteen,' I say quietly.

'Mmmm.' She lays her palm on my back and I close my eyes at the incredible softness of her skin.

She reads aloud the Russian words. *Oh Lord, forgive me for the tears of my mother.*

I twist around and grab her wrist. 'That's enough.'

Something flashes in her eyes, but it's not fear.

'So now you know all about me,' I say. 'What is there to know about Tasha Evanoff?'

'There is only one thing you need to know about me. Tonight I am yours.'

'Let me see what is mine tonight, then,' I say.

Pink rushes up her neck and cheeks. She sinks her teeth into her bottom lip and holds her empty glass out to me. I take it from her and she steps out of her shoes. How cute. No other woman I know would dream of taking her shoes off first. Every one of them is sophisticated enough to know a naked woman wearing nothing but her high heels is the ultimate sexual turn on.

She takes her cardigan off and folds it before laying it neatly over the edge of the couch closest to her. As her hands move to the back of her dress, I see them shake and realize she is nervous as hell. She unzips her dress and lowers it slowly. Underneath is only the lacy white bra. She doesn't try to fold the dress as it pools around her ankles. Swallowing hard, she removes her last item of clothing and lets it drop to the carpet.

And I behold a body of classical proportions.

My fingers tighten around the glasses in my hands. A word I don't think I have ever used comes into my head. Willowy. Her breasts are small and round, the nipples pink and erect, and her waist gently flares out into delicious curves that part into slender thighs. And between them pink folds protrude.

Other than the hair on her head she is completely hairless. Her flawless pale skin shimmers gently in the soft light. There is not a single mark on her body. As if she never fell over as a child and grazed her knees or hurt her elbows. Lost in awe I drag my eyes back to her face.

Anticipation and excitement have made her eyes glitter a brilliant blue. Here she is, on the wrong side of respectability, with the baddest of the bad boys. A dangerous, cold-blooded killer. It is in her eyes: the good girl is expecting a dirty, thrilling, wild, forbidden night of lust and passion.

A night like no other.

And she will get it.

Looking into her shining eyes, I remember the birthday present Vasily and the rest of my staff gave me. It was meant to be a joke. Like a blow up doll only better. Much better. Even I had been surprised by how incredibly real it looked when they presented it amongst blankets, but I never thought I'd have use for it.

Until tonight ...

I scoop her up, she weighs so little. I carry her upstairs and lay her on the bed. She looks up at me with huge eyes. She appears so innocent and beautiful I almost cannot bear to look at her. The simple truth is I cannot bear to return her tomorrow.

I feel anger grow from deep inside me that she cannot be mine. Not just for tonight, but forever.

I've always wanted her, and now I'm being offered one little taste before she is yanked away and given to a bully who does not deserve her.

I already know what he will do. He will break her with neglect.

She, who is mine.

Five

Tasha Evanoff

https://www.youtube.com/watch?v=FK6
wgua-kjc
Everything Is Not Quite Enough

Lying naked on the bed, I watch him walk shirtless, the muscles of his inked back gleaming, to the attached dressing room. I see his reflection in a mirror open a cupboard and from the top shelf take down a large package. He brings it to the bed and puts it next to me.

'Open it,' he invites softly.

I sit up, curious, and open the plastic packaging. I stare at it, surprised and slightly confused.

'It's an authentic, life-size vagina and ass,' he explains the obvious from above.

'It's a masturbator for men,' I say slowly. Worrying at my lower lip I look up at him. 'What are you going to do with it?'

He smiles slowly. 'Not me. You.'

I stare at him. 'Me? What am I supposed to do with that?'

'I want to see you suck that pussy.'

'You want me to suck a plastic pussy?' I repeat in disbelief. This was way too kinky for me

'It's not plastic. It's a CyberSkin deluxe version. Touch it.'

I look down at it then back up at him. 'I'm sorry but I'm not into women. Not even a bit.'

'Touch it,' he urges.

'I—'

'I want you to.'

'Fine.' I touch one of the butt cheeks and it feels surprisingly real and soft. I retract my hand. 'Yeah, good, really lifelike, but what's the point? It's not doing anything for me, and quite frankly I'd rather taste you.'

'It's the visual for me, but the elemental taboo for you.'

I look at the thing. It basically looks like a woman's hips and thighs when she is lying face down and sticking her ass out so that her vagina projects out with all her frilly bits distended.

'Let me show you how easy it is,' he says, taking hold of me in a flash, opening my legs with his powerful hands, and staring down at my exposed sex. Like a man in a trance, he kneels between my legs. His head moves downward and his lips connect with the throbbing at my core. I jump as if I have been electrocuted.

He lifts his head. 'Relax,' he orders.

I stare at the ceiling, furious with myself for reacting like a frightened rabbit, or some little Victorian virgin prude. I'm going to make this night work. One way or another. I've dreamed of it too long not to. He buries his head between my thighs.

'Oh, God,' I groan, my body arching involuntarily, when his tongue finds the wet opening and plunges inside. The pleasure is delicious.

His hands roam my body as his tongue swirls inside me, licking, rolling, slurping, tasting my depths, eating me as if he is a starving wolf. My legs lock round his head and my pussy tightens around his eager tongue. Just when I think he has found the right spot he goes deeper, or shifts the angle, and finds a whole new right spot.

'Yes, there,' I cry, my whole body bucking as I grind my sex against his mouth and chase my orgasm. When I am almost screaming with pleasure, he removes his tongue from inside me and clamps his lips around the small hard bud of my clit and suckles it.

'I'm so close,' I moan.

His reply is to suck harder.

'Oh, Noah,' I scream and, grabbing his head, come. Hard! The world becomes white with the intensity of my climax. It is beyond anything I have experienced before. The orgasm rips through me and leaves me a quivering mess and I become aware that his tongue is still lodged inside me.

'That was amazing.' My voice is hoarse.

He lifts his head, his mouth and chin glistering.

'You're amazing,' he says and dips his fingers into me. I gasp and tighten my muscles around the digits. With wide eyes I watch him gather the juices from my pussy and smear it on to the vagina of the toy. He even inserts his fingers into the toy to coat the insides.

I meet his dark, inscrutable eyes, and suddenly I want to be the girl who is so wild and willing she is extraordinary. I know he will haunt me forever. Let it not only be him that leaves an indelible mark on me. I'll give him a show he will never forget.

I get on my knees and sink down on the toy's frilly pink lips. I lick it and, for the first time, taste my own juices. On my knees and sucking a toy pussy smeared with my own juices, I hear him draw in a sharp breath. In my peripheral view I see him take his trousers off. I want to see his cock, but he moves to the back of me. I slurp at the lips greedily, and exactly as he had done to me, I dip my tongue into the soft opening.

Behind me I hear the sound of a condom wrapper being hurriedly torn open and my whole body becomes electrified. Every atom alert and waiting for his touch. First those large, rough hands wrap around my hips, then, his cock head starts to penetrate me. I am dripping wet, but it is enormous and I cry out with pain as it spreads me open and forces itself into me. I feel him stretch me wider and wider as the hard pillar goes deeper inside me. As I start to adjust to the thick cock inside me, the sensation of fullness is wonderful.

This is what my sex was made for.

'Spread your legs wider,' he instructs, his voice thick with lust.

I obey.

'Wider still and push your ass up,' he commands.

With my pussy speared with his cock, I can't help the feeling of being helpless and vulnerable. My entire body prepares itself to get the fucking of its life. I whimper as the nub between my legs begins to throb like a heart. I know then that I want him to start moving so bad it feels as if I will break into a thousand pieces if he does not.

He begins by rolling his hips, slowly, deliberately, before picking up speed, bumping into me as far as he can go and feeling so big inside me. The thrusts becoming more savage, building and building to an almost unbearable speed. Mercilessly he fucks me as fast as he can while my hips rise up to meet his thrusts.

Until every nerve ending in my body is screaming for release.

'Play with yourself,' he growls.

I use my fingers and frantically frig at my clit and almost instantly I feel a monster orgasm coming my way.

'Stick your tongue into that pussy while my big cock fucks you,' he orders, and suddenly I'm riding an enormous wave. He must have been holding back and waiting for me because he roars and explodes together with me.

My climax begins at my core. It blasts through my body like a firebomb and ends at my fingertips and toes. The power of it turns my cry soundless and makes me physically shake. I didn't know where I ended and he began anymore. We were one, one never-ending earth-shattering climax.

Every time I think I have reached the edge, this must be it, there cannot be more, Noah carries on jackhammering the entire length of his cock deep into my body, and it begins all over again, the next climax slamming into me like a brick wall. Until my brain feels fried, my mouth is screaming noiselessly, and my limbs shake and convulse uncontrollably.

Nothing I have ever done, not by myself, or with any other guy compares to this mind-blowing sensation.

When it is finally over, my body feels as heavy as lead and I am so completely drained my upper body collapses on the bed. His hands don't let go of my hips. He keeps us joined while my pussy carries on convulsing and gushing around his cock. Only when all the tremors are gone does he pull out of me.

He falls to the bed, his head appearing next to my eyes. I turn to look at him with awe. 'Is it always like that with you?'

He shakes his head, his eyes mysterious.

My hand reaches out to touch the masculine lines of his face. 'You really are so beautiful,' I whisper.

A ghost of a smile crosses his face. It's an oddly bleak smile. It makes me want to hold him close to my heart and never let go. To my surprise, my eyes fill with tears. I'm not normally a crybaby.

His eyes narrow. 'What's the matter? Did I hurt you?'

I bite my lip to stop the sniffles. 'No. It's just the emotion you released, I guess.'

He nods.

'You don't say much, do you?'

Six

Noah Abramovich

She is nothing like I'd imagined. In my mind, I deliberately painted her as a spoilt Princess. Rude, uncaring, cold, shallow, carelessly whiling away her time the way the daughters of very rich men do, an army of trailing servants to pick up after her. Even so, I wanted her badly, but now that I have drunk her sweet nectar, I crave her the way a man dying of thirst craves a glass of cool water.

'You don't want to talk to me?' she asks, her eyes clouding over with hurt.

Fuck. How can a grown woman be so innocent, so fucking clueless about what a man wants? Can a woman like this ever fit into my fucked up life?

What the fuck? Did I actually entertain that crazy thought in my head? *Goddamn you, Noah, you're just screwing with yourself. You can never have Tasha Evanoff.* Her father would rather boil me alive than let the likes of me have her. Hell, he'd have boiled me alive if he knew I even touched her. I feel a twitch start up in my jaw. The rage of being so close to something you are dying for and knowing you can never have it.

'What do you want me to say, Tasha?' I ask harshly.

Her eyes widen with shock at my bitter tone.

'In a few hours you'll be gone forever. What should I say? That was great. Thanks. Or better still, want me to say I'll fight for you? I'll kill your father, the man you're supposed to marry, and anyone else who stands in my fucking way.'

Her lower lip starts trembling. She presses her mouth into a straight line, turns away from me, and stares up at the ceiling.

'You don't have to be so horrible. We are just ships passing in the night. You are a man. Surely you must have had many such nights as this. Were you this horrible to all of them too?' Her voice breaks on the last question. She blinks hard and fast, but a tear slides out from the corner of her eyes and runs down her temple into her hair.

The sight makes my chest hurt. Something inside me feels like it is breaking. I cannot understand how she can so easily get under my skin. I am the tough guy. No one gets to me. Ever. Yet, I am like putty in her hands. I get up onto my elbow and very gently lick the salty stream.

'I'm sorry.'

She fixes her gaze on me, her beautiful, beautiful eyes piercing my soul. 'It's okay. I forgive you. I never want to fight with you,' she murmurs.

Her quick acceptance of my apology is child-like and endearing. With every second that passes she entwines herself more and more tightly around my heart. I touch her belly and her hand runs down my body and cups my still half-hard cock. It starts to swell and she smiles, feeling powerful, knowing she is the cause.

She lifts off the bed and I watch as she drops to the floor and, bending her head, fills her mouth with the broad mushroom head of my cock. Her mouth is heaven, soft, warm and velvety. Slowly, she slides her lips just over halfway down my cock, and my long shaft is already at the back of her throat. She begins a smooth cock-sucking rhythm. A nun with a toothache could have done better, but her inexperience and inability to take the whole of me excites me so much I feel my climax already building. I sit up, pull out of her mouth, and enjoy the exquisite sensation of sliding my cock along her tongue.

'Get on your knees,' I tell her.

I stand and angle her head so that her neck is arched back. Then, with my fingers tangled in her hair, I guide her head so I slide back in. I push my cock all the way to the back of her throat, slightly further than before. Her eyes widen with panic, but I hold her head there, and obediently she remains. I enjoy the moment of total control. Of having Tasha Evanoff's mouth at the end of my cock.

Pre-cum must have touched her throat because she swallows. I pull out, and I watch her take a deep breath and I know I can't last much longer. I want my sperm in her throat and in her belly. I pull her face against my throbbing cock as it clenches and tightens. Then I am gone, spurting hot cum down her throat. Spurting and spurting and watching her swallow it all. Every last fiery drop.

I made Tasha Evanoff drink my cum.

I look down at her, her eyes wide, her succulent mouth gently sucking the last drops of cum from my dick. The tension leaves my body. I made her submit to me. A woman who will continue to suck your cock after you have come inside her mouth is a woman who belongs to you.

I pull out of her and, grasping her by the upper arms, pull her onto the bed. She stares up at me while I start worshiping her body the way I have never done another woman. She is pure woman. Pure ecstasy. Her taste and the strong sweet smell of her arousal make my mouth water. I lick and suck, nibble, bite and stroke every inch of her. I suck her pink nipples until they swell to almost twice their size. The more she begs me to enter her, the more I torment her.

'Take me,' she begs lewdly, spreading her legs and showing me her engorged, shining pussy. I lift my head to enjoy the sight. Her whole body spasmodically jerking, hot, wet, and surrounded by her halo of gorgeous hair.

'Please,' she begs pitifully.

41

'Fuck me, Noah. Fuck me.' Her hips thrust helplessly at thin air. It gives me a cheap thrill to hear her use the word fuck.

'Say fuck my cunt,' I order.

She doesn't hesitate. She is too far gone. 'Fuck my cunt,' she cries.

'Please ... Noah ... please.'

But I carry on tormenting her until her hips are jerking and her thighs trembling uncontrollably. Then I stop.

'Now you may have your release, but you'll have to work for it yourself,' I tell her as I lie on my back. I let my eyes roam her body. Covered in saliva and aching to be filled with my cock, she crawls towards me and swings one leg over me.

'Stop,' I demand, and she freezes, her pussy garishly gaping open and glistening, her face contorted with frustration.

I commit to memory the dirty image of Tasha, no longer a Princess, but horny, slutty, her leg cocked over my dick, and out-of-control sexy.

'What?' she groans.

'Now,' I tell her.

She immediately impales herself on my meat until I'm completely buried in her tight pussy. Mewling and squirming

with relief and pure sensuality, she rotates her hips and grinds her pussy on my pubes. Her eyes are closed and I see the bliss in her face.

When she starts rocking back and forth, I gather her close to me and suck on her puffy, reddened nipples. When she utters a low cry of pain and pleasure, I begin to suck voraciously at the enlarged tips. As I bite down on one, I thrust the fingers of my other hand between her lips, forcing her to suck her own juices.

'Bounce on my cock,' I growl.

She tightens her pussy muscles and lifts herself upwards two or three inches, but my hands on her hips pulls all but my cockhead clear out of her, followed immediately by my cock slamming back inside her.

'Talk dirty to me.'

She licks her lips and looks at me with half-hooded eyes. 'I'm a dirty slut. Give it to me hard and fast!'

'Fuck yeah.'

'I want you to put your big cock in my mouth and let me suck it until you fill my belly with your cum.'

Of course, she would have to be a fucking natural at this too.

 43

'Not just my mouth. I can't wait for you to fill every hole in my body with your hot cum.'

She keeps at it, and I start to slam harder and harder into her sweet cunt until we slam right into the hurricane of our climaxes.

Seven

Tasha Evanoff

'**A**re you hungry?' he asks.

I grin at him. 'I thought you'd never ask.'

He grins back and I stare at the beauty of the man. I have never seen him smile with his teeth showing before. He is spellbindingly handsome.

Unaware of my appreciation of him, he jackknives upright and, naked, walks to the dressing room. He comes back wearing track bottoms and holding a shirt in his hand.

'Wear this,' he says, holding it out to me.

I slip into it and fold the sleeves up.

He gazes at me.

'What? What are you thinking?' I ask.

'How fuckable you look.'

I blush and he laughs.

45

'Come on,' he says leading the way. We go downstairs in our bare feet.

'What's there to eat?' I ask, sliding onto one of the creamy yellow stools. His kitchen looks like it is hardly ever used. Every surface is gleaming with newness.

'I don't know,' he says opening the fridge.

'You don't know. Who does the shopping for you?' I ask curiously.

'I have a woman who stocks my fridge and my cupboards.'

I get up and join him in front of the fridge. We study the contents together. His fridge is well stocked with unopened packets of food. Fresh vegetables, salad in a plastic bag, cheeses, meat, fish, jars of condiments and containers of cooked food.

'You've got *Khachapuri*,' I exclaim, my stomach rumbling at the thought of the crusty bread shaped to look like a boat, the middle filled with different types of melted cheese and baked with an egg thrown on top of all that cheese. Mmmm ...

'Shall we have one?' he asks.

'One? I'm not sharing my *Khachapuri*. Get your own.'

46

He grins down at me and for a second there is something soft in his eyes, then it is gone and replaced by something slightly distant and unreadable.

'Fine, we'll have two. I was just thinking you might want to save some space for the *Morozhenoe*,' he explains in an amused voice.

'*Morozhenoe*?' I echo, my eyes bright. I love creamy Russian ice cream.

'Uh ... huh,' he says, taking two portions of half-baked crusty bread filled with cheese and putting it on the granite counter top.

'Oh my. A midnight feast with *Morozhenoe*. I used to have it direct from the carts whenever I went to Moscow. Now that I know you have it, I'll have to come here more often,' I say with a laugh, and suddenly realize what I have said.

There is no expression on his face as he unpacks the bread. 'Do you want yours with an egg on top?'

'Yeah,' I say softly, walking back to my stool. Somehow the mood has been ruined.

I watch him crack two eggs on top of the bread boats and put them into the oven. He has big powerful hands. There are stars tattooed on them. I think of those strong, tanned hands on my body and the thought arouses me, makes me want him inside me all over again.

'You don't cook often, do you?' I ask.

'Almost never.'

'So what happens to all the food if you don't eat it?'

He shrugs carelessly. 'I think Irina takes it home.'

I nod, my body going cold. When I asked him for one night it never even crossed my mind that he might have a girlfriend. Just because I saw him alone all the time I just naively assumed that he didn't have one. Have I just had sex with someone's boyfriend?

'So who's Irina?' I ask as casually as I can.

He frowns. 'Sort of my housekeeper.'

'Sort of?'

'It's complicated.'

'Complicated as in girlfriend?'

He looks surprised. 'No, I'm not with anyone,' he says.

Getting information from him is like squeezing blood from stone, but it is a strange relief to know there isn't a girlfriend lurking somewhere. He pulls open the freezer and takes out a bottle of Tovaritch vodka. My father's favorite. Putting my elbows on the smooth cold surface and supporting my jaw in my palms, I watch him pour us a couple of shots.

He brings them to me.

'I don't want to get drunk,' I say.

'Want a raw egg?'

It is a Russian tradition. If you don't want to get drunk have a raw egg before you start drinking. I shake my head.

'Drink it in one go and don't exhale through your mouth,' he advises.

'Got it,' I say and take the glass.

'*Vsego khoroshego*!' he says.

For a second I hesitate. That phrase can mean all the best or goodbye.

As if he has understood the reason for my hesitancy. 'All the best,' he says in English.

'All the best,' I echo. It had not felt right. The thought that he might have been saying goodbye. I down the drink. It slides smoothly down my throat.

He opens the oven and the delicious smell of bread baking fills the kitchen. We sit and eat. He seems to watch me eat more than he eats.

'Are you not hungry?' I ask.

'I'm hungry, but not for food.'

When I finish, he scoops ice cream into bowls. 'If only we had some chocolate pieces to sprinkle on top,' I say as I stuff my face with soft creamy ice cream. He gets up and opens a cupboard, rummages around and finds chocolate sprinkles. 'Will these do?'

'Okay,' I say.

When I lay down my spoon, he comes over to me. He grasps my waist as if I weigh no more than a child, and puts me on the granite top. The stone is cold under my thighs.

'My turn to eat ice cream,' he says.

The ice cream is cold and I do giggle to start with, but not for long. He ruins ice cream for me forever.

Eight

Tasha Evanoff

'What time is it?' I ask.

He swivels his head at the alarm clock by the bedside. 'Nearly four.'

So the night is all gone and it is almost time to leave. I sigh.

'Can I use your shower before I go?' I ask softly. I reek of sex.

'Sure,' he agrees. 'There's a clean bathrobe hanging behind the door.'

He watches me get out of bed. I walk away feeling sore between my legs. The bathroom carries the same décor as the rest of the house. There is a pale pistachio wall with a massive mirror encased in an ornate creamy lemon frame. I use the bathroom, ooh, sore, and get into the shower. I switch it on and adjust the temperature setting before I step into the rush.

I close my eyes and turn my face up to the water cascade. I try not to think. It

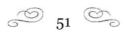

cannot be over. Our time together flew by too quickly. How could something so wonderful be over? Suddenly, I become aware that the shower door is open. I twist around and Noah steps into the cubicle.

I watch the water pouring down his face.

He doesn't say anything, but simply puts his hand to the back of my head and swoops down on my mouth. Unresisting, I flow into his arms, my body yielding to the hard planes of his. His insistent mouth parts my shaking lips and sends wild tremors through my body. The rest of the world falls silent and becomes nothing while I cling to him as the only solid thing in my shifting world.

The whole night he has avoided kissing me and I thought it was because he didn't want to, but this kiss is hot and full of a kind of wild desperation. Like a condemned man who decides to gamble his life on a game of Russian roulette.

His tongue invades my mouth and I suck on it.

He pulls away from me and we stare at each other. His eyes are blazing and his jaw is clenched so tight I feel a spark of

fear. Before I can ask him what is wrong, he turns away and walks out of the shower cubicle.

Wrapped in his bathrobe I venture cautiously into the bedroom. He is not there, but he has brought my clothes up and laid them on a throne-like red velvet armchair. I dress quickly. He has also put a hairdryer out and I use it. I pick his hairbrush and run it through my hair. It feels strange. I have never used anyone else's brush in my hair before. Probably because I've never been allowed to stay at a friend's for a sleepover, or pajama party.

Stepping in my shoes I go downstairs. He is in the living room, holding a glass of something amber.

'Thanks for bringing my clothes up,' I say shyly.

He lifts the glass in my direction in acknowledgment of my words.

'I guess I should be going.'

'I've called someone to take you back,' he says quietly.

'No, that won't be necessary. I really should call a taxi.'

'You're either leaving with my guy or you're not leaving at all. Take your pick.' His voice is hard and unyielding.

'Look, if I happen to meet someone I know, it is better if I am in a taxi. I don't want to get anybody in trouble.'

'Don't worry. Sam will be driving a taxi.'

'Oh, is he a taxi driver?'

'No.'

'Right.'

'Do you want a drink?'

I shake my head. 'I want to keep my wits about me.'

He nods. 'Good idea.'

'I've had a ... really good time. Thank you.'

He drains his glass and pours himself another. He downs that one too and stares at me as he does it.

'What time is Sam coming?' I ask, fidgeting nervously.

'Soon.'

'Okay. I'll have a glass with you.'

Silently he pours us both a drink and brings mine to me.

'We should drink to something.'

He raises a cynical eyebrow.

I raise my glass. 'Here's to happy lives for both of us.'

'Happy lives,' he echoes, an odd edge to his voice.

We knock it back. He turns away from me and walks towards the bottle.

'What will you do today?' I ask into the awkward silence. He is so distant, so cold, it is impossible to imagine that it is the same man who licked ice cream off my body while I giggled like a schoolgirl. Or the man who came into the shower and kissed me like I was the most precious thing he'd ever had.

He shrugs. 'Sleep. You?'

Talk about short answers. I can play the same game. I grimace. 'Boring stuff.'

His phone vibrates and he goes rock still. Something happens inside my body when I watch him pick it up and put it to his ear.

'Yeah, she'll be out now,' he says.

I want to touch him. I want to kiss him. I want our goodbye to be different. I feel ... oh, God ... I can't ...

I don't want to leave him.

Nine

Noah Abramovich

https://www.youtube.com/watch?v=jqp
AgMxhx30

Once the taxi has driven off, I close the front door and walk into the living room. The house feels like a fucking tomb. No wonder I never come here. This is a family home. It is meant to be filled with the sound of a woman and children. Not this deathly silence.

I have the urge to smash something. I pick up the glass I left on the coffee table and throw it blindly. It crashes into the wall and smashes with a resounding noise. Then the silence returns. I press the heel of my palm into my forehead. Damn it. Damn it.

This can't be fucking it.

No fucking way.

I stride to the bottle of cognac and pour myself a large measure. I drink it so fast the liquid burns my throat, but on an empty stomach it is finally starting to dull off the sharp edges. I sit down on the couch and pour myself another. Tasha Evanoff. My limbs feel heavy and dead. I grasp the bottle by the neck and take a long swig.

Ah, fuck it. She's just a woman.

There is a Chinese saying. People are like a finger in water. Take the finger out and the water closes over seamlessly. Not even the memory remains. No matter how important they seem to be their absence doesn't count a damn.

I look at the dent in the wall. It is some kind of specialist paint or shit. I'll have to get that annoying designer back in here. A thought crosses my mind and I go into the kitchen. I stand at the doorway and look at the counter smeared in ice cream. I see her again, spread out on my dark granite completely coated in the oozing sweetness, squirming, laughing, a creamy sticky mess.

I see me bending down to slowly lick the drips from her breasts, her stomach, my tongue exploring everywhere, every inch, pretending I was not really in search of the sweet nectar between her legs. More ice cream lands on her giggling body, more licking, until she didn't squirm or giggle anymore.

I turn away from the empty counter. I have never felt so alone in my life. I sit on the couch and pull my feet up. Not long before daylight. She would have arrived at her home by now. I call Sam.

'All done,' he says crisply.

'Where did you drop her off?'

'One street away.'

'Right. Thanks.'

I drink until I can't see straight, but the wanting doesn't go away. I can't face the bed. I close my eyes and sleep comes. I wake up at the sound of someone in the kitchen. My head is hammering. I look at the bottle rolling on the floor. It's empty.

I groan when Irina comes into the room.

She is coming into the room bringing a small saucer. '*Nikolashka*,' she says. Her voice rings like a fucking Church bell in my head.

It is an old Russian cure for a hangover. A slice of lemon with a teaspoon of sugar and a teaspoon of coffee on top.

I shake my head and pain shoots into it. '*Nyet*,' I whisper.

'It's either this or *haash.*' There is not an ounce of sympathy in her voice. Fuck that. *Haash* is a Caucasus thick stew that is prepared by cooking tripe and beef trotters for six hours, and to make it worse, it is consumed with radish and lots of garlic. I'd rather die than let one drop of that shit into my mouth.

I put my feet on the ground and a bolt of pain hits my brain.

'Fuck,' I curse, cradling my head.

Irina stands patiently next to me with her saucer.

I reach out a hand, take the lemon slice and, sliding it between my dry, crusty lips, chew it slowly. As soon as I have swallowed it, she nods with satisfaction and goes back to the kitchen. I stand up slowly and go straight into the bathroom. I switch on the shower and stand under the hot jet. The sluggish blood in my veins starts pumping. I roll my neck and stretch the knots from my shoulders. Last night feels like a dream. I get out of the shower, brush my teeth, and walk naked to the bedroom.

Slivers of sunlight slanting in through the window shutters make me squint. My eyes turn to the unmade bed.

She was no dream. I walk to the bed and, grabbing a fistful of bedding, pull it up to my nostrils. Her smell clings to the bed sheets like early morning fog across a lake.

I can't just let go of her like that. She belongs to me.

I go to the window and pull the shutters open. Bright yellow sunlight blinds me for an instant, then I see them. An Omen. In my head Babushka is saying, *eto magiya* (it's magic). Two blackbirds have settled on the pillars on either side of my gate.

A dormant memory, fresh as if from yesterday, fills my mind.

Babushka's hands with their bulbous knuckles are moving quickly. She is peeling red onions to make pickles for the winter. It always makes the whole house smell of vinegar. Around her head is the triangularly folded headscarf and I am reading the newspapers to her. Suddenly a bird flies in through the open window and perches on the inside ledge.

'Look, Babushka?' I gasp.
She looks at the bird.
'What kind of bird is it?' I whisper back.
'It's a blackbird,' she says and smiles.
'Is it a good omen?' I ask curiously. Babushka assigned meaning and superstitions to even the smallest occurrences.
She throws a peeled onion into the bucket and picks up another one. 'All the birds that wear robes of black come to tell us the seeds of change have been planted in our lives. Often they bring news of death because that is the greatest change of all.'
'Who will die in our house?' I whisper aghast.
'No one. When you see a blackbird you must smile. Tis a great blessing. It is an early warning. Telling us to be prepared. To love those around us even more deeply than we think is possible because one day they will be no more.'
She smiles at me and I smile back.
'Now sing,' she says.

And I sang for her. I was eight years old.

That winter was the first time I knew Mama was ill. That time they cured her. The next time the illness came back I would be thirteen and this time she would suffer for two years two months and five days before she left Babushka and I forever.

For a moment I just stand and watch silently. What seeds of change have you brought? What do I have to be prepared for? Who do I have to love even more deeply than I think is possible before they are taken away from me forever?

I don't move but they must have sensed my figure because they look up towards me before they simultaneously fly away. I draw myself away from the window and Tasha Evanoff fills my head.

Her luscious curves, warm sweet breath and eyes full of simple joy. No matter how much I try to make myself believe last night was nothing more than two animals acceding to their wildest, lustful desires, I know different. I also know slow darkness will follow after taking the forbidden. But I don't care. I shrug a shoulder.

I've waited for a long time to make that pussy cry out for me and fuck me it did, over and fucking over. Hell, I can't remember the last time a woman made me feel this alive. I drag myself back to the bed, my cock stiff and throbbing with blood surging from my brain. I get in and grasp its thickness firmly. With long slow strokes, I visualize that sweet pink flesh that drove me to such wickedness hours earlier.

I see my cock power into her, thrusting mercilessly, as savage as the Alpha wolf with his female. I took her like it was my last day on this earth. What a fucking glorious ending! My free hand grips my chest and my heartbeat rises as my orgasm begins to race forward like an unstoppable freight train.

Oh, fuck, oh, fuck me. My cock pulsates, frantically cheering my hand on, like it has a fucking mind of its own. I stroke faster and faster, and feel the perspiration form across my forehead. My whole body stiffens as I shoot my hot seed into the air.

Fuck. Fuck you Nikita Evanoff.

This, this is just the fucking beginning ...

Ten

Tasha Evanoff

I stand a block away from my home. I look around me and there is no one. It's still early and no one actually walks the streets in this neighborhood. There is a nip in the autumn air, but I am warm in the butter-soft, brown leather jacket that Noah insisted I wear.

'I can't be seen in it,' I told him.

'Then ditch it before you get home,' he replied carelessly.

I stood still while he helped me into it. He lifted my hair out of the collar and zipped me up as if I was a child. Then he stepped away from me and let his hands drop to his sides.

'So it's goodbye,' I said, wanting desperately to prolong those last moments.

He didn't answer. Just nodded and opened the door, his hand clutching the handle so hard his knuckles shone white.

I didn't want to go, but my legs moved and I walked over the threshold, down the steps, and straight into the cab. I smiled automatically at the man called Sam as he shut the door.

As he got into the driver's seat I turned my head and looked at Noah. His tall frame filled the doorway, still, dark and mysterious. I lifted my hand and waved, but he did not wave back. Then the cab began to move and I wanted to scream for him to stop, to take me back where I belong.

But I didn't.

I just sat in the cab, numb and silent, until we were nearly at my house. That's when my sense of self-preservation kicked in and I leaned forward and told Sam to drop me off a block before my house.

'Just there, by that post box would be great.'

That's how I come to be standing a block away from home hugging Noah's jacket. A cold October wind ruffles my hair as I take the first step towards the place I call home and my legs work. I take another step and another step. With every step my body starts rewiring itself. I

did what I wanted to, and it was the most beautiful fantasy I could have dreamed of, but now it was over, and real life had to begin again.

When I am half a block away I take the jacket off, but I cannot bring myself to throw it away. I roll it up into a ball and walk a bit further down the road. My hands are itching to throw it away. If I get caught … there will be hell to pay for not just me, but Noah too, but my heart won't let me. It is the only thing I will ever have of him.

As I get to my best friend Lina's house, I pop into her front garden and stuff the jacket in the blue recycling containers left outside. It must be collection day. I know the trucks don't come until mid-morning. I'll either come back in a couple of hours and retrieve it, or I'll just call Lina and ask her to keep it for me until later.

When I get closer to the house I take out my mobile phone and call my grandmother. Although it is five-thirty in the morning, she answers her phone on the first ring and sounds completely alert. My grandma wakes up at four every morning to do her prayers. She prays for hours for my father's soul.

'Tasha,' she says.

'Baba, can you give me a hand?'

For a moment she is silent. Then she exhales the breath she is holding. 'Of course.'

I walk to the wall at the back of the house and wait across the road. The gates have CCTV cameras running 24 hours a day, but the walls only have cameras that swivel on a 180% arc. So if you time your journey to or from the wall carefully you will never appear in it. I wait, half hidden by a cherry tree. Five minutes later a rope comes over the wall and I run to it.

I have less than 45 seconds before the camera will return to that spot. I run across the road and climb the ladder nimbly. I have been doing this since I was six years old. I jump onto the springy grass and pull the ladder up behind me. I carry it with me and run to the ancient Yew tree. Less than ten seconds left. I reach into the roots of the tree and pluck the rope out of the metal hook hidden within. I yank it but it gets stuck.

Shit.

Five seconds left.

 67

I get on my haunches, untangle it, it comes off, and I heave it free. Clutching the ladder and rope to my chest, I roll on the ground and get behind the tree. I push myself upright and lean against the back of the tree. My heart is hammering and adrenaline is buzzing through my veins, but I'm smiling. Three Rottweilers are licking my hands and face.

I made it.

I speak softly to them, patting their muscular, well-trained bodies, and fishing little treats from my cardigan top to give to them. 'Go on. Off with you,' I tell them, and they trot off to resume their guarding duties.

I stand up and wait for the camera to do its complete sweep before I run back to the house. I throw the rope ladder back into its black bag and dust myself off. Thank god, it is not raining. Although I have made this trip in the rain, I would have made a right mess of myself, rolling on the wet ground. Carrying the bag, I walk coolly into the kitchen.

It is empty, but for Baba. She is sitting at the kitchen table wearing the thick housecoat she wears to bed and a dressing gown over it. Her short, coarse iron-gray hair is uncombed, and her face is pale without her lipstick. There is a pot of tea and two cups and saucers laid out on the table. I walk up to the table and, dropping the bag on the floor, sit in front of her. Silently, she fills the cups with tea.

'Isn't the appointment for your wedding dress fitting today?' she asks in Russian. Baba is the only one who speaks to me in Russian.

'Yes.'

'At what time?'

I look down at the steam rising from my tea. 'Half past eleven.'

She pushes the container of sugar towards me. 'Where have you been?'

I look into her deep set, dark eyes. They're similar to Papa's in coloring, but while his are cold and dangerous, grandma's are warm and full of concern.

'I was with a man,' I confess.

Eleven

Tasha Evanoff

A look of deep sorrow and fear comes into her eyes. She clasps her pink, shiny hands on the table top because they have started trembling.

I love my grandmother and though I knew she would not approve, I never expected to see her look so desolate or frightened for me. It's not like I've hurt anybody. I just took something for myself and I have been careful not to cause consequences to anybody. I reach for her hands and cover them with mine.

'Oh, Baba, please, please, don't be sad or scared,' I plead. 'Nothing bad happened and nothing will. I wanted him for a long, long time and I would have always regretted if I had not taken this night for myself, but now I've had him I can move on. I can put it all behind me and be a dutiful daughter to Papa.'

She blinks slowly. 'You wanted him for a long, long time?' she echoes in a daze.

'Yes, for a very long time.'

She shakes her head in disbelief. 'Have I not known you at all, *Solnyshko*?'

'You've known all of me, Baba. This is just something my heart wanted.' I smile. 'It's like how you sometimes still crave for your babushka's *smokva*.'

'*Smokva*? Yes, we called it dried paradise apple in our village,' she says, her eyes misting with the memory. 'It was very precious, but I have never crawled over a wall in the middle of the night, or … risked a man's life for it.'

I take my hands away from hers. 'Papa will never find out.'

She shakes her head. 'You could have been caught. Someone could have seen you.'

'No. I was very, very careful. I told no one. Not Mama, not even you.'

She sighs sadly. 'Do you know *smokva* originally meant dried figs, but because they were too expensive for the ordinary person, somebody had the idea to boil up locally available apples, quinces, plums and rowanberries in honey or sugar syrup? *Smokva* was the poor man's substitute for figs. You don't need to make do with a substitute, Tasha. You can have the real thing.'

I stare into her eyes and whisper, 'That was the real thing, Baba. That was the real thing. What I will have after him will be the substitute.'

Her eyes widen and she gasps. 'Who is this man?'

'You wouldn't know him.'

Her eyes narrow. This is when she looks closest to Papa. 'But my son does?'

I nod.

She draws her breath sharply. 'This man, will he tell, boast to anyone about you?'

I shake my head. 'He's not a kid. He understands it could cost his life.'

'And he will not try to make trouble?'

I shake my head again.

'Will you see him again?'

'No,' I say and it is a wretched sound. I can see that it startles my Baba. 'It was just the once,' I say miserably, 'so I'd know what dried figs taste like.'

'Oh, *Solnyshko,* you don't know what you have done.'

'I have done nothing. It was just this once. I did it for me. My whole life has been one long Lent and just this once I indulged.'

'You think you have had one taste of carnal pleasure and now you can walk away and never look back? You have only awakened the demon of desire.'

We are both staring at each other when the door to the kitchen suddenly opens. Both of us jump and swivel our heads towards it. Papa is standing at the doorway. He is still dressed in the clothes he went out in last night. My father is a balding, short, barrel-shaped man. If you saw him in the street you wouldn't even notice him, but if ever you chanced to look into his black eyes you would shudder with something unnameable. Like looking into the eyes of an insect. Not evil. Just soulless. This man could kill a man with the same emotion with which he sneezes or takes a piss.

His cold, pitiless eyes narrow at the sight of us: my grandmother in her dressing gown and me all dressed as if to go out or ... no, the thought will not even occur to him that I could engage in a dirty stop out night. Surreptitiously, slowly, I push the black bag with the rope ladder deeper under the table.

'Good morning, Papa.'

'Why are you dressed at this time of the morning?' he asks, a frown marring his forehead.

'The child has her first wedding dress fitting this morning and she is so excited about it she woke before the birds were up.'

My father's face relaxes. He turns to me. 'Who are you going with?'

'Lina.'

'Good.' He comes into the kitchen. I stand and, walking over to him, dutifully peck him on his cheek. He smells of alcohol and perfume, a strong cloying scent. It makes me step away from him quickly, afraid that he will smell Noah on me, but he absently rubs his cheek where I have kissed him, and turns to look at his mother. When I was younger, I thought he didn't want me to kiss him, and he was actually rubbing away the kiss, but when I stopped kissing him the next time I saw him, he looked at me with his cold eyes and asked me why I did not kiss him. 'Never forget to kiss your Papa,' he told me sternly.

'Vasily is coming from Moscow this afternoon,' Papa tells my grandma, 'and he is bringing *Ptichie Moloko* from The Prague restaurant for you.'

Ptichie Moloko or Birds' Milk Cake is made from French marshmallows and chocolate and set on a cake base. It is the king of all Russian desserts and Baba's favorite.

Grandma keeps her eyes on me while she smiles, but her smile doesn't reach her eyes.

'Oh good. No one makes it like they do at The Prague restaurant. All the rest are plastic imitations.'

A dull heat spreads up my throat and into my face. My father looks at me. 'You're blushing. Why?'

I swallow hard.

'Leave the child alone, Nikita. She is excited about her appointment,' Baba says reaching for her cup of tea. She sips the cold liquid calmly.

Papa just grunts.

It never fails to amaze me the tone my grandmother uses on her son. This is the man who makes grown men shiver. He has never raised a hand to me. He has never needed to. The only time I saw something cruel and frightening in his face was when I came home from school and called him Daddy. Like all the other children in my school did. His head swung around so fast it was like the strike of a snake.

'What did you call me?' he asked, so softly I felt goosebumps rise on my hands. Anyone would have thought I'd used the f or the c word.

I thought he must have had misheard. 'Daddy,' I repeated.

'I'm not your daddy. I'm your Papa. Don't ever try to be like those miserable creatures you go to school with. You can mix with them and pretend to be one of them, but never forget you are Russian and only Russian. You have my blood in your veins. Never let me hear you exchange your culture and your Russians ways for theirs again.'

He had totally discounted my English heritage. The blood of my mother. Of course I never said anything. My mother tells me. Let sleeping dogs lie. Wake them up and they will bite you.

'Yes, Papa,' I said immediately, and since then I have never done anything that has earned that soft, menacing tone from him again.

The kitchen falls suddenly silent.

'It's been a long night. I'm going to bed,' Papa says into the strained silence.

'Sleep well, Papa,' I say, and step forward to kiss his cheek again. My father reaches out a hand and plucks a one-inch-long twig from the elbow of my cardigan and drops it to the ground. I freeze with fear, but he doesn't realize the significance, and turns towards the door. I watch him go out of the door with relief and hear the sound of his shoes on the marble floors echo through the empty house.

'I suppose I better go to my room as well. Sergei will be waiting,' I tell my grandmother.

She nods.

I bend to pick up the black bag and she grasps my hand suddenly in hers. The steely strength of her grip surprises me and my eyes fly to meet hers. Something strange and dark lurks in them.

'*Solnyshko*, if you ignore your dreams they will limp away from you to die a sad death,' she warns urgently.

Twelve

Tasha Evanoff

Moving through the high-ceilinged, gilded, pillared excesses of my father's home, my heels clicking on the marble, and the relief of not being discovered gone, I feel oddly hollow, as if I have left an important part of me back in Noah's home.

I go up to my room, open the door, and immediately my beloved four-year-old blue Doberman, Sergei, rushes over to me and throws his sleek body at me. I crouch down to have my face and neck thoroughly washed, but he suddenly stops and sniffs me curiously.

'I know,' I whisper. 'I've been with a man, a beautiful, strong, powerful man.'

Sergei stops sniffing me and licks my face gently, as if he understands that I am sad and lost. I hug him tightly.

'Oh, Sergei, Sergei, what am I going to do? I never thought it would be like that. I thought I had built it all up in my mind and it would fall flat. He would be a selfish brute, but he was just beautiful. Just beautiful. Indescribably beautiful.'

I lie on my bed, Sergei's head on my stomach, while my mind replays last night. I think of Baba's expression when she grasped my hand and told me ignored dreams die sad deaths. I think of my father's chilling eyes and then I think of Mama.

When I was five years old my parents separated, no, that would be giving the wrong impression, that the decision was in some way mutual or amicable. Nothing could be further from the truth. My father kicked my mother out. Literarily opened the front door and kicked her out so she fell sprawled on the front door steps. He spat on her and forbade her to ever see me again. He did all this with me watching and screaming with fear while Baba held me in her arms. I still remember Mama, getting up to her feet, her knees were bleeding, but she was staring at me, desperately memorizing my face, when the door shut on her.

He did all that because he suspected her of being unfaithful to him. Of course

it was not true, but my father was, is, and will probably always be highly paranoid. Every shadow is a Judas waiting to betray him, steal from him, plot his murder. He even did a paternity test to confirm that I really was his child. And since then Papa has been married three times. None of them could bear him any children. He divorced the first one. I think she went back to Russia. She hated me and I didn't like her. The second one was more cunning. She made a huge pretense of liking me, but disappeared one day. I don't know whether she ran away because she was so afraid of my father, or my father did away with her. Papa's third wife died in a car accident. Brake failure. When he was informed of it, he nodded slowly, then put another forkful of calves' liver into his mouth. We went to her funeral dressed in black. Nobody shed a tear.

After my mother went I cried for days. I never stopped begging Baba to let me see my mother. At first she told me to forget Mama. Mama had left the country.

'But where could she have gone? All her clothes and shoes are here?'

'You can't see her. The sooner you accept that the better it will be for everybody.'

'I'll run away,' I threatened.

'There are bad men outside these walls. They will catch you and do terrible things to you.'

'Can't you ask Papa to bring Mama back?' I begged.

'No, *Solnyshko,* I can't.'

But I wouldn't relent. I was determined. Every day without fail I begged her. Sometimes I wouldn't even eat.

Then one day she took me shopping and we 'accidentally' bumped into Mama. Oh the unexplainable joy. I can still remember how I would wrap my arms tightly around her neck and howled when it was time to part. Then Mama started crying and Baba scolded me.

'If you don't stop that we'll never be able to see Mama again.'

Every time I turned back I would see her standing where we left her, watching us sadly until we turned a corner, or the crowd swallowed us.

In the car, Baba cautioned, 'Remember you can never ever tell anyone about this. If you do you will never see your Mama again.' Her eyes stared at me earnestly. 'And perhaps not even me.'

My mouth opened in horror. 'Will Papa kick you out of the house too?'

'Perhaps,' she said softly.

From that day on I learned to be ultra-secretive. To keep my mouth shut. To watch everything that came out of it.

As I grew older, Baba taught me how to use the rope ladder. Ever since then I have been using it to go visit my mother.

Sergei suddenly lifts his head, jumps off the bed, and goes to scratch at the door. I let him out and call Lina. It is nearly nine o'clock.

'What?' she says sleepily.

'Hey,' I say. 'I ... uh ... left a jacket in your recycle bin. Would you mind very much putting it into a bag? I'll pick it up from you when we go to my fitting appointment.'

There is a slight pause. 'A jacket?'

'Yes, a brown leather one.'

'In *my* recycle bin?'

'Right,' I confirm.

'Uh ... huh. Am I going to get any kind of explanation?'

'Um ... not, right now.'

"Fine, go ahead and be mysterious, then.'

'It's important.'

She sighs. 'What do I do with it again?'

'Just bring it with you when we go for our appointment.'

'Okay. What time are you coming?'

'About ten thirty.'

'Are you excited?'

'Yeah, sure. Sure, I am.'

Thirteen

Tasha Evanoff

Lina thanks Anatoly, our driver, and slips into the back of the car next to me. She thrusts the John Lewis plastic bag at me as Anatoly closes the door behind her and goes around to his seat.

'Thanks,' I say air kissing her cheeks.

'No problem,' she says. Lina is American. She has a thick head of shining, chestnut hair, chocolate eyes and a blood red mouth. She gets her dusky coloring and her sultry looks from her Italian mother.

'Are you excited?' she asks with a grin.

'Yeah,' I say, trying to inject enthusiasm into my voice.

'So, you want to tell me about the jacket?'

'Not just yet.'

'Okay. I was under the impression there was a fairly innocent explanation behind it, but now I'm having to revise it up to scandal category.'

I squeeze her. 'I'll tell you later. I promise. We'll go somewhere for tea and cake.'

'No, not cake. I'm on a diet.'

I smile faintly at her. I've known Lina since kindergarten, but I've never truly confessed my secrets to her. Sometimes I would make things up so that it did not seem as if it was always she who was telling me things, pouring her heart out to me while I was holding back. Even when I became engaged to Oliver, I never told her how I really felt. Always at the back of my mind, Baba was saying, The less you say, the safer you and they will be.

It is only a short journey to Wardour Street, where Valeria Lahav, the most famous Russian bridal dress designer has her studio. The first to get out is Vadim, my personal bodyguard. He walks to Valeria's black door with its gold knocker and rings the bell on the side.

When Valeria answers and her receptionist comes to open the door, he comes to the car and holds open the door, Vadim returns to the car and holds the door open for us. Afterwards, he positions himself outside the closed door.

Valeria comes out to the reception area to greet us. She has curly blonde hair that is in a messy ponytail at the back of her head and she is smiling widely at us.

'You are going to be so pleased. I can't wait for you to see it. The dress is more beautiful than I thought,' she gushes.

I smile politely and follow her into the large room. There is a long wooden table and a few tailors' dummies in one corner. She positions us in front of a curtain. 'Are you ready?' she asks theatrically.

'Yes,' I say with a big fake smile.

She pulls the curtain and I hear Lina gasp beside me. It is certainly not modest. Then again, Valeria's designs are famous for their extravagance and intricacy. Italian ivory lace over light gold featuring a high mandarin and yards and yards of silk tulle skirt. There are Swarovski crystals delicately sprinkled throughout with rich decorative beading at the empire waist. I stare at it with conflicting emotions. I have to admit the dress is stunning, extravagant, intricate and more beautiful than I ever imagined when Valeria and I first discussed it and she showed me her sketches and swatches, but I don't want to marry Oliver. Not in this dress, not in any dress.

'All of this,' she is saying, 'is hand finished by the top seamstresses in Russia using the finest luxury sewing techniques. All the stitches are so tiny you cannot see them without a magnifying glass. Come and see the back,' she encourages.

I walk around it, noting its keyhole back and the fishtail train finished with scalloped edging.

'The zipper closure is hidden with silk-covered buttons,' Valeria says proudly.

I nod automatically.

'It's absolutely mind-blowingly gorgeous,' Lina says.

'It's lovely,' I murmur.

'Are you ready to get into it?' Valeria says.

Her assistant comes and they carefully help me into the dress. I stand on a raised round platform as still as a statue as they do their thing. Lina is sitting on a chair, watching. She doesn't say anything.

'That's it. All done,' Valeria declares.

They ask me to turn around and look into a large mirror on the wall. I look at my reflection. The dress will cost in the region of £45,000 and it is undoubtedly very, very beautiful, but I simply don't look like a radiant, blushing bride. My eyes are dull and I can barely bring a smile to my face. I can see that Valeria and her assistant have both realized that the appointment is not going as swimmingly as they thought it would. They think they have done an amazing job, and they have. Lina strolls over to my side.

'Do you mind if I have a moment with Tasha?' she asks Valeria.

'Of course not,' Valeria says, and quickly bustles out.

Lina stands in front of me. 'You don't want to get married, do you?' she says slowly, her eyes filled with a sick realization that everything I was doing was a lie.

I shake my head slowly. I can feel tears burning at the backs of my eyes. Before last night, I don't know how I did it. Maybe because I so desperately wanted to, I had somehow managed to persuade—or rather trick—myself into thinking I could do it. I could live that loveless life. I could be a good wife the way I was a good daughter. I would pour my love on Sergei and my kids when I have them.

'Why?'

'I thought I loved him,' I lie.

'Don't lie to me. Please. You think I didn't know about all those other times you were lying? I just let it go, but not this time. Just tell me the truth for once.'

I shrug and look down.

Her mouth falls open as the realization dawns. 'Oh my God. You're doing this for your father!'

I don't say anything.

'This is completely crazy. This is the kind of thing they did in the 18th century. What? You're just supposed to marry a man you don't have any feelings for because your father tells you to?'

'It's not like that. It's a mutually beneficial alliance. My father has money. His family has the title and the right social circle. It will be good for everybody.'

'What about you? Hmmm?'

'It will be good for my children.'

'To be in a loveless relationship?'

'To have the advantages that his family name will give them.'

'From what I can see all these lords and ladies are all fucked up, stuck-up, weak motherfuckers. Give me a commoner any day. Do you really want that for your children?'

The tears that I have been holding back leak out.

'Oh fuck,' Lina says and starts rooting around in her bag for some tissue. She finds one. It's scrunched up and has lipstick stains on it, but otherwise it looks clean. I take it and wipe my eyes.

'So what's with the leather jacket?'

'It belongs to someone I spent last night with.'

'Fuck me ragged!' she breathes, then laughs. 'It's always the quiet ones you can't trust.'

'Oliver is not faithful to me and he doesn't care if I sleep with other people either. He once told me that if I wanted to have affairs after we are married I am welcome to it, as long as I follow two conditions. Ensure I do not get pregnant and I am very discreet.'

'See what I mean about them being fucked-up.'

I smile half-heartedly.

'So tell me about this guy then,' she urges. 'Who is he?'

'You don't know him and it's better if you don't know who he is. The less you know the better it is for you.'

Her eyes become wary. 'What's really going on, Tasha? Are you afraid? Because you're fucking scaring the shit out of me.'

'I'm not scared and I'm not trying to frighten you. It's a truism in my father's world. The less you know the safer you are.'

'Fine, don't tell me who he is. Was it good? Did he have a big dick?'

In spite of myself I smile. 'Yes, it was very good.'

'And the dick?'

'Yes, it was big,' I admit with a giggle.

'So what happens now?'

I sober up again. 'Nothing.'

'Was it just like a one-night stand?'

'Yeah, something like that.'

She looks at me curiously. 'Why is it, it feels like more?'

'It's not more, Lina. It can never be more.'

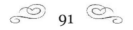

'How does he feel about you?'

'It was just a sex thing for him. I offered myself to him on a plate. Of course, he took it.'

'Tasha, sometimes you say some really dumb things. Just because a woman offers herself on a plate doesn't mean the man is going to take it. You were obviously to his taste. Did he say or show any signs that he wanted more?'

I press my hand into my midriff. 'It was a one-night stand, Lina, and anyway my father would not approve of him. He would consider him beneath me.'

She opens her mouth, but I interrupt her by saying, 'Don't say it. Just leave it, and let's talk about something else.'

She looks at me as if she pities me, but she changes the subject. 'What are you doing tonight then?'

'I have that Alexander Malenkov charity do. Remember, I'm on the organizing committee. I sold most of the tickets. You didn't want to come.'

'Yeah. No thanks. I would have gone if Mr. Malenkov wasn't already married. The man is totally fuckable, but since he is there'd be no point. You know me and classical music are like oil and water.'

I smile at her. 'It's a party, Lina. As of last night there was one last ticket left. Why don't you come?'

'You're going with Oliver, right?'

'Yes. Will you come?'

She sighs.

I sense she is weakening. 'The food is from the L'Auberge Du Pont de Collognes of the Paul Bocuse Group,' I pause for maximum effect, 'the only restaurant in the world to retain its three Michelin-star status for fifty years.'

She hesitates.

'They're serving Kaluga Queen Caviar, 1.8kg per table, and Snow Leopard Vodka.'

She has the beginnings of a grin on her face. 'Hmmm ... Snow Leopard Vodka, huh?'

'Uh-huh. Made from rare spelt grain from one of the world's finest distilleries,' I add hopefully.

'You really want me to come, don't you?'

I look at her and suddenly realize that I do want her to come. I need someone beside me who knows how I really feel. 'Yes, I do.'

She smiles. 'Okay. It better not be filled with crusty old men, or you'll owe me big time.'

'I think it's going to be filled with crusty people.'

'Oh well. There's always the bar. Five Sex On The Beaches later every man starts to look a bit like Henry Cavil.'

'Thank you so much,' I gush gratefully. 'Quick, pass me my phone.'

She gives it to me and I call the girl in charge of tickets.

'Oh dear, I'm so sorry, Tash. I'm afraid you're too late. I just sold the last ticket this morning.'

'Oh, never mind. If one comes up will you please reserve it for me and call me?'

She assures me she will and I end the call.

Lina touches my arm. 'You'll be fine. With or without me.'

Fourteen

Tasha Evanoff

I get out of the car and Oliver lets his eyes roam greedily over my body. I am wearing a long, black, halterneck fitted dress with a slit on one side. 'You look fabulous,' he compliments. 'But then you always were a bewitching little fox.'

'Thank you,' I say quietly.

'How did your dress fitting go today?' Oliver asks as we arrive at the iconic Pavilion of the Tower of London. The historic walls of the tower are lit up, and I pull my gaze away from the impressive sight and let it focus on Oliver.

Oliver has the quintessential aristocratic face. His father is a Marquis and he is a Lord by birth. His family have a vast estate with one of the most beautiful stately homes in Britain. I have been to Moreland Abbey. It is truly magnificent, but the family lives in a small section of the house because the rest of it is crumbling, leaking, and too expensive to heat. Marrying me means they will be able to refurbish their ancestral home and bring it back to its former glory.

I plaster on a smile. Fake, of course. 'Good. The dress is very beautiful,' I reply as I cross the threshold of the venue and into the reception area. The guests are already milling about in groups holding drinks in their hands.

He winks at me. 'Did you ask her to leave a secret opening for me?'

My stomach churns and I struggle to swallow the hot acid rising in my throat. I look at the bar longingly. I need a drink. Tonight is going to be a long night. I bring my gaze back to his leering face and smile apologetically. 'No, it was not really an option. It's got a big skirt.'

'Right. One of those mafia virgin bride jobs, is it?'

My smile drops. This is not the first time that Oliver has made this kind of remark. They are supposed to pass off as jokes, but in actuality, subtly or overtly, let me know my genealogy is less illustrious than his.

'I don't know what you mean,' I say stiffly.

His leer loses some of its shine. 'Does it have one of those big skirts that I can just flip over your back and fuck that beautiful ass of yours?'

I feel the color drain from my face. 'It has a big skirt, yes,' I say quietly.

'Good. We're in business then.'

We reach the cloakroom and I check my coat in.

A woman in a tight black dress and an impressive butt comes to stand next to us and Oliver's eyes openly linger on her buttocks. She turns and looks first at him then at me.

I pretend not to notice. The girl behind the counter gives me my ticket and I turn towards Oliver. He brings his gaze back to me. 'I'm going away to New York for a week.'

'When?' I ask softly.

'Next Thursday. It's business. Your father will be there too.'

I knew that my father was going to New York, but I did not know that it was with Oliver. 'Who else is going?'

'Just Elizabeth.'

'I see,' I say. Elizabeth is Oliver's secretary and his lover. Elizabeth doesn't even bother to hide the fact. Twice I have met her, and both times she has made it patently obvious that she is giving him what I am not. I want to look her in the eye and tell her that she is not so special after all, she is not the only one. He has others too.

Once, when we were out at a restaurant, a woman passed our table. She gave him a funny look. Less than a minute later he excused himself to go to the toilet. I waited a few minutes before I followed him and saw them in the corridor leading to the toilets. Her breasts were pressed into his chest and his hand was rubbing her ass. I walked back to the table and never said a word. I understood that it would be the pattern of our lives together. He will always cheat on me. Possibly it cannot even be called cheating because he is so open about it.

Oliver leads me towards the white, minimalist bar. On the way we meet people he knows and he stops to chat, his hand hooked loosely around my waist. 'Have you met my fiancée, Tasha Evanoff,' he introduces proudly.

Everybody is polite, but everybody is always polite to your face at these occasions. Behind my back there are always whispers about how my father's great wealth was acquired. They are more correct than they realize.

When we finally get to the bar I would love to order a shot of Vodka, but I don't. I do the civilized English thing and get a vodka and soda. Other people come to join us, and it is a relief because it means I don't have to talk, I can just stand there nodding and flashing a polite smile at appropriate moments.

https://www.youtube.com/watch?v=BT4GIljqr-A
Can't Take My Eyes Off You

Finally, it is time to go through the double door into the massive, regal dining area. Gorgeous sapphire-blue lights lend a romantic, glamorous hue to everything they touch. The green carpets look sea blue, and the canopy ceiling is full of little light reflections that create the stunning effect of stars glittering in a summer night sky. The tall candelabras

on every table hold aloft orangey red cups of light.

Our table is close to the stage and midway between the entrance and the dance area. We take our seats and the Queen caviar is brought to the table on dry ice. I throw back the Vodka and let the salty bubbles explode on my tongue as we listen to the speeches from the patron of the charity thanking the sponsors of the evening.

My father didn't come, but he is one of them, and since I am his representative, I smile and nod when his name is mentioned and the camera pans on me. After a slideshow depicting the different projects the charity has undertaken to help the disadvantaged children of Russia, it is time for the highlight of the evening.

The curtain draws open and the spotlight falls on Alexander Malenkov, the object of Lina's unrequited lust. I have never heard him play, but the moment he touches the keys the entire audience falls so silent you could have heard the proverbial pin drop. He plays with great passion and true skill and I must admit I am awed by his performance. When he plays his last note and stands to take a bow, all of us spontaneously give him a standing ovation.

The curtains close on him and food is served. The food is delicious of course, but I find myself pushing the food around my plate and pretending to eat. I keep thinking that this is what my life is going to be after I marry Oliver. An endless string of the same type of empty functions with the kind of people I have nothing in common with. After I have play-acted consuming the dessert, the last event of the night begins.

The Precious Items Auction is where the guests take off their jewelry or personal items like watches and wallets, and give them up to be auctioned. The items are not collected beforehand, but donated on the spot together with the little receipts that have been left on each table describing the item in as much detail as possible for the auctioneer together with a suggested starting price.

One of the ladies at our table bequeaths her pearl necklace, another offers her rose-gold bracelet, and I take off my emerald and platinum earrings and place them on the platter.

The auction starts with Lady Schloss's Cartier watch. On the screen behind the podium, a blown-up 360° image of the watch is shown. The starting price is £2,000.00. After a lively bidding it goes to her husband for £5,700.00. The same process is more or less repeated for nearly every woman who gives up her jewelry for auction. Her husband or fiancé ends up winning it back for her. It is all good-natured fun and a bit of charity included.

Then it is my earrings.

'Kindly donated by Miss Tasha Evanoff,' the auctioneer announces. 'A pair of perfectly cut, flawless Brazilian emeralds set in platinum. Each perfect emerald is 4.5 carats.'

He lifts his hand.

'Let's start the bidding of at £5,000. Do I hear any takers? Yes, we have. To the gentleman at the back. At the side here. £5,500. Do I hear £6,000. Yes, we have £6,000. £6,500. £7,000 to the gentleman at the back. £7,500 to the gentleman in the red tie over at the side. £8,000. We have £8,500. This is a rare opportunity to buy a truly exquisite pair of earrings. £9,000. £9,500. £10,000. £10,500. Come on ladies and gentlemen. This is all for a good cause. Well done, we have £11,000 in the front. Anymore bids?'

He looks around hopefully.

'Going once. Going twice.' He nods at Oliver who has just raised his hand. 'Thank you, Sir. We have £11,500.'

I smile sweetly at Oliver. All eyes are on us and we are both playing the part of a couple deeply in love.

'Any more bids for this rare and magnificent pair of earrings?' The auctioneer raises his hammer. 'Oh, looks like a new bidder has entered the fray. £12,000.'

Both Oliver and I turn around to look at the new bidder and I freeze. My stomach drops. I cannot believe my eyes. Noah is sitting at Alexander Malenkov's table.

Sweet Jesus. He is the one who bought that last ticket this morning!

There must have been a reshuffling of the table seating. Someone on the table must have exchanged places with him. Our eyes meet. And I can't tear my eyes away. Lost in his gaze I don't even hear the rest of the world.

Then I see him lift one finger and I hear the harsh indrawn breath Oliver takes. I tear my eyes away from him and stare unseeing at the drama unfolding on the stage.

£13,500 becomes £15,000. £15,000 becomes £20,000. £20,000 becomes £25,000. I feel Oliver shifting with irritation beside me. He doesn't want to lose face, but the price will soon become too high for him. With a tight smile he nods, and nods, until the auctioneer's hammer hits the gravel at £75,000!

Noah has won the earrings.

Oliver pretends to smile graciously. He is actually shaking with fury. He turns to me and kisses me on the lips, slowly and leisurely. His mouth is cool and smells of the orange liqueur drizzled on his chocolate dessert. When he takes his mouth away my gaze flies helplessly towards Noah. His eyes are blazing and his jaw is clenched so tight there is a white line around his mouth.

I drop my eyes. Over on the stage, the next item is being described by the auctioneer. My stomach swims as I turn blindly towards the item being displayed.

After the auction, they give away awards to some people who seem very grateful to receive them, then the dance floor lights come on and the DJ introduces himself.

I quickly excuse myself to go to the Ladies. As I get to the corridor, I see Noah leaning against the wall. He is with a woman, a beautiful redhead. It makes me want to gag. I can't. I can't even look at them together. The thought of him doing to her all the things he did to me is unbearable. It's like molten lava pouring in my gut. Oh God. I spun a spider's web of lust for myself. Now I sit trapped like prey in its silken ropes. As I stand there burning, rooted to the spot, he sees me, excuses himself, and walks over to me. His stride is relaxed and prowling.

My knees are trembling.

Fifteen

Noah Abramovich

I notice her engagement ring immediately. It's a dazzling thing. Big, ostentatious, and fucking ugly. She didn't wear it last night when she came to me. I fight the urge to rip it off her fingers.

'Fancy meeting you here,' I say.

'I thought all you had to do today was sleep,' she taunts, but her voice shakes.

'I thought all you had to do was boring stuff.'

She bites her bottom lip. 'Did you know I would be here?'

'What do you think?'

'How did you know I'd be here?'

'Let's just say I'm a friend of Alexander and I knew you were in the committee organizing this event.'

Her eyes widen. 'You know Alexander Malenkov?'

'Sure. I used to work for him.'

She can't imagine how I might be connected to a world famous pianist and her smooth brow knits. 'Really? As what?'

'It's not important. It was a long time ago.'

'Oh. Why did you bid for my earrings?'

'Why does anyone do anything?' I can't get the image of him kissing her as if he owned her out of my mind.

'You did it to make my life a little bit more miserable.'

'No,' I say harshly. 'I bought them because you belong to me. Every woman in that room had her jewelry bought back for her by her man. That was my right. I'm your man.'

She looks at me with wide, wretched eyes.

The question slips out before I can stop it. 'Are you sleeping with him?'

She shakes her head.

'I want to see you again.'

She swallows hard. 'I don't know. That was not part of the plan.'

'Fuck the plan.' My voice is harsh.

'You don't get it. My father will have you killed if he finds out about us, and the more times I see you, the bigger the risk that somehow he will hear about it.'

'Come to me tonight.'

'Did you hear what I said?'

'I'm not afraid of your father.'

Her eyes widen. 'You should be. He is a very dangerous man.'

'I'll be waiting for you.'

'I can't. I—'

'There you are, darling. I was wondering where you'd got to,' Oliver says smoothly. He turns towards me. I feel him sizing me up. 'Aren't you going to introduce me to your ... friend?' The pause is not lost on me.

'Lord Oliver Jarsdale, Noah Abramovich. Noah Abramovich, Lord Oliver Jarsdale,' Tasha says. There is a guilty tremor in her voice and I feel him stiffen with suspicion and anger.

'Ah, another Russian,' he says, and there is a wealth of meaning in his words. A deliberate snub, which surprises me because from what I have heard, Jarsdale is one of those slippery men who doesn't insult you to your face, he'll do it behind your back anonymously. My manager has a good term for that phenomenon. Twitter balls.

He looks at her, his nose raised as if there is an offensive smell about. 'A friend of your fathers?'

I feel Tasha's whole body contract. I know she never wanted me to come to her father's attention.

'Actually, he is a friend of Alexander Malenkov,' she says, her words stumbling over each other.

Something cold flickers in his eyes. 'And how do the two of you know each other.'

'We are old friends.'

'Really?' he drawls. 'How interesting.'

I smile as casually as I can. 'Yes, we Russians all tend to know one another.'

'It would seem so,' he says in a tone of someone who is suddenly bored by the conversation. 'Anyway, we should be going. Enjoy your earrings, Mr. Abramovich.'

I say nothing.

'Nice seeing you again, Noah,' Tasha says softly. Then Oliver places a possessive hand on the small of her back and leads her away. My gut burns with jealous fury, but a cold logical voice inside me says, *Look around you Noah. This is*

*not the fucking place or time. Let him
think he's won.*

I stride out of the venue and go stand
outside. I light a cigarette and take a drag
on it. What I really want to do is go back
inside and choke the fucking breath out
of Jarsdale. Someone comes to stand next
to me. I don't have to turn to know who it
is.

'You're asking for an all out war,' he
says in Russian.

I take my box of cigarettes and offer
it to him. He takes one and I hold the
flame of my lighter under his cigarette.
He cups his hands around the flame and
inhales. The fire illuminates his face and
long, elegant fingers. Strange, all those
years not once did I see these digits as the
fingers of a gifted pianist. He lifts his
head and I withdraw my lighter.

I've loved this man like a brother for
years. We've seen each other through
thick and thin. Everybody calls him
Alexander now, but to me he will always
be Zane, my brother in arms.

I take a drag of my own cigarette and
exhale it. 'I'm not afraid of him.'

He blows a puff of smoke out. 'If I was a betting man I'd have to put my money on him,' he says quietly.

I turn to look at him.

He meets me in the eye. 'Simply because Nikita is hindered by neither fair play nor honor. While you are still pondering the ethics of killing the father of the woman you want, he will bury you.'

I frown. Zane is right. I've thought about it and I can't inflict any kind of hurt on her.

'What you did today was reckless. If you truly want this woman, don't let your dick think for you again.'

'I'm not letting my dick think for me. I shook the tree. I wanted to see what fell out.'

'Nothing good can fall out of this tree. What's your plan?'

'Stay out of this, Zane. This is my affair. You're out of this cesspit. Stay out. Take care of your family.'

Sixteen

Tasha Evanoff

Oliver curls my hair around his index finger. 'Why do you think that Russian gangster wanted your earrings so much?' His voice is soft, but hostile.

I look at him with surprise. 'I don't know, but why do you care? I thought you didn't mind what I did as long as I was discreet.'

In his eyes something ugly rears its head. 'To start with, it doesn't look like you have been too ... discreet. It doesn't take too many brain cells to figure out what was going on tonight.'

He smiles nastily.

'Secondly, I might have been a bit hasty. I didn't care then, but since then I have become rather ... fond of you, and I certainly don't appreciate another man throwing it in my face that he has got into your pants.'

My skin crawls, but I resist the intense urge to edge away from him. 'What are you saying?'

'I suppose I'm saying the rules have changed. From now on I expect my wife to be faithful to me.'

I look at him coldly. 'And this rule is obviously only applicable to me, since you are obviously not faithful, nor do you plan to be anytime in the future.'

'Play your cards right and that could be arranged,' he lies, his lips grazing my neck.

I close my eyes. I've got to do something fast about this situation I'm in. I can't go on like this. I know now that I could never have sex with Oliver. Maybe before, but not anymore. Not when I am in ... love with Noah.

'You don't love me and I don't love you,' I say softly.

'What's your point?'

'Should we really be getting married, Oliver?' I coax. If I could just get him to call off the engagement there won't be a thing Papa can do.

He looks at me strangely and then bursts out laughing. 'Are you getting cold feet? Let me tell you, sweetheart, it's much too late for all that.'

'No, it's not.'

'Aww ... you really thought you could persuade me to break off the engagement. Sorry, no can do.'

'But you don't really want me.'

He smiles strangely. 'On the contrary, sweet Tasha, I very much want you.'

I stare at him in horror. 'No, you don't. You have other women.'

'They are bodies. Bitches and prostitutes. I can barely remember their names. No, Tasha Evanoff, you are the prize.' His lips twist. 'I choose you to be my wife and the mother of my children.' He takes my wrist and suddenly crushes it.

'Owww, you're hurting me.'

He squeezes harder and I grit my teeth. 'Did you imagine ours will be a marriage in name only?' he taunts.

I stare up at him defiantly.

'I will fuck you hard and often. As of today I expect to be the only cock going into your tight little cunt.'

I gasp in shock.

'You can tell that Russian dickhead that his little performance has just made your life that much more complicated. Tell him to bang good and proper now, because I expect purity from my wife. So if you are getting any smart ideas of taking on lovers, I should warn you now that I'll put a fist through your lusty hole before I allow that.' He makes a fist with his hand. The gesture is violent and lewd.

I become rigid with shock. This is a side of Oliver I never suspected.

'Have I made myself clear, or do you need a demonstration of what to expect?'

I stare at him in disbelief and he grabs my hip and pulls me towards him, his erection pressing into my belly as his hand goes up my skirt. Suddenly, I wake up from my daze.

'Yes, yes, I understand,' I whisper urgently, my voice shaking with fear.

He tightens his hold on my hipbone until I cry out in pain. With a taunting little laugh he lets go and I close my eyes, swallow hard, and try to calm myself. I open my eyes and he is watching.

'You really are very, very beautiful, Tasha. So white and perfect.'

115

Seventeen

Tasha Evanoff

By the time I get home the fear has receded to the back of my mind. As soon as I open the front door, Sergei, who is waiting patiently for me, goes mad with joy. His excited yelps and barks echo loudly in the mausoleum-like-silence of our house.

'Let's go see Baba,' I say.

He licks my face.

I stand up. 'Race you,' I challenge, and start running up the stairs, but he overtakes me easily and waits for me at the top. I tickle him behind his ears.

'You win,' I concede.

He nuzzles the back of my knee. With him following at my heels, we go down the corridor.

As I have done ever since I was a child, I don't knock but simply enter. In my life Baba is the only open book. I have seen her naked, I have seen her sick, I have seen her cry. When she fell and broke her hip, I didn't want her to be embarrassed by the nurse or maid changing her nappies or cleaning her up so I did it all myself. She never hides anything from me and I don't either. Not for any length of time, anyway.

She is already in bed reading a book. She peers at me from over her glasses and smiles. 'What a lovely surprise, *Solnyshko*? Did you have a good time tonight?'

I go and sit on the side of her bed and Sergei curls up at my feet. 'Yeah, it was okay, I guess. I auctioned my emerald earrings and they fetched £75,000 for the charity.'

'Who bought them?'

'Guess?'

'A frog would turn into a hog faster than Oliver would pay £75,000 for a pair of earrings so it won't be him,' she deduces shrewdly.

'You're right. Oliver was outbid by someone else.'

Her eyes widen slightly. 'Well, well,' she says softly.

I stare at the pretty little piece of nail art on my big toe before looking up at her. 'Baba, I need to go and see him tonight.'

She takes off her reading glasses, closes the book, and puts it on the bedside table.

'Say something, please.'

'What can I say, *Solnyshko?* Forbidding you to see him will only fan your desire to see him even more.'

'It's not just desire. I miss him, Baba. I miss his voice, I miss his face, I miss his touch. I even miss the sound of him breathing. He's waiting for me. I have to go see him. I'll go mad if I don't see him tonight.'

She looks at me anxiously. 'It is dangerous for you to be out alone this time of the night. I cannot condone such risky behavior.'

'Baba. There are so many security guards outside every house on this street that it must be the safest place on earth.'

'Still,' she says, her eyes full of worry.

'Even before I get to the main road a minicab will be waiting for me. I did it yesterday and it was fine.'

'What if it is not fine today?'

'Oh please, Baba. I'll be careful. I promise I'll be very, very careful.'

She sighs heavily. 'I'm not happy about this, *Solnyshko*, but go with God and don't be careless. You hold so many people's lives in your hands. It's an ugly world out there and the consequences of your actions could be great.'

I stare at her. 'There won't be consequences. I just want to see him one more time,' I cajole.

She smiles sadly, because we both know I am lying. There will be consequences. I'm planning on changing everything. One more time? A three-year old kid can see through that piece of fiction.

'Your father has gone out, but I don't think he will stay out all night so be very careful. No matter what time you want to come back in just call me.'

'I won't wake you until after four.'

'I can sleep anytime. Call me when you are ready.'

'Thank you, Baba.'

'Wear your jeans today. The weather forecast said it might rain tomorrow.'

I grin at her. 'Did you know I'd go to see him?'

She grins back. 'If I was your age, I would do the same.'

I laugh. 'Can I leave Sergei in here? I don't want him to be lonely two nights in a row.'

'Of course. Bring his bed in here and put it over there by the wall.'

I stand up and kiss my grandmother's cheeks. When I am very close to her ears, I whisper, 'His name is Noah.'

'It's a good, strong name,' she whispers back.

'I love you,' I say, and run out of her room.

In my own room I change quickly into jeans, a T-shirt, and sensible shoes. I find a cardigan and throw it over my T-shirt. Then I fill its pockets with dog treats. Standing in front of the mirror, I take down my hairdo and tie my hair into a ponytail instead. I make the bed with the pillows arranged to look like a sleeping person, then I call the minicab company and arrange for them to pick me up in ten minutes at the end of my street.

I look around me. Everything is as it should be. I pick up Sergei's bed and his toys and call to him. 'Come on, you're sleeping with your grandma, tonight,' I tell him. He looks at me reproachfully so I hug and tell him that one day, one day, I will take him to meet Noah.

Switching off the light, I close the door and go back to Baba's bedroom. After I have settled Sergei and bade my grandma goodbye, I run downstairs. The house is quiet and still, and the soft soles of my shoes make no sound as I go out through the side door that locks after itself. I walk quickly towards the back of the house. The Rottweilers come to me, triggering the security lights; they make quiet whining noises.

'It's only me,' I tell them, giving them little liver treats.

After I have sent them away I watch the moths fly towards the bright security lights. Just before they switch off, I start to count the seconds for the camera to come back around. The lights die and I carry on counting the seconds.

When I have counted enough time for the camera to do its sweep of that patch of ground, I run to the wall and, stepping into the grooves in it, climb over it. I drop onto the other side as nimble as a cat (I have been doing this for many years) and casually walk down the road. The taxi with the minicab company's name printed on the door is waiting for me at the end of it. I open the door, slip into it, and give the driver Noah's address.

My heart is hammering in my chest.

Eighteen

Noah Abramovich

There is beauty in everything.
All you have to do is open up your heart
-Mahinour

There are no stars in the night sky above, and the air is strangely heavy and full of static electricity. A storm must be coming. I stand in my back garden smoking a cigarette, my whole body tight and strung out. It is waiting for hers.

For so many years, I dreamed of her. I dreamed of conquering her, fucking her, branding her, pulling the stuck-up Princess's hair, forcing her to take my cock, and seeing her on her knees cowed and submissive. All it took was one night. Just one night for her to turn my dream to ashes.

If I was a tree, I lost, leaf by fucking leaf.

The tip of my cigarette glows amber as I inhale deeply. I look at my watch. It's already twelve thirty. She won't come tonight. It is too late. The disappointment is like a crushing weight on my chest, but I tell myself it is for the best. It disturbs me to think of her taking a taxi at this time of the night. The world is a cruel place for a beautiful woman.

I flick the cigarette away and roll my tense shoulders. Her black velvet box of earrings is burning a hole in the pocket of my pants. I take it out and open it. The jewels gleam in the light from the open doors. I tilt the box and they catch the light and look like green fire. I stroke the stones. They don't feel cold to the touch.

I have never done anything like this before. Always kept my emotions locked away. Nothing but ice-cold concentration for the job at hand. Maybe I shouldn't have bought them, but at that moment I couldn't bear for him to claim her as his. She belongs to me and she will be mine even if it is the last thing I do.

Filled with a deep sense of restlessness, I close the box and drop it back into my pocket. I don't want to get drunk alone again. I should go out.

Maybe I'll go to the club and have a drink with the boys, though the prospect doesn't enthuse me.

I start when I hear the doorbell ring.

I turn to the sound, staring through the French doors. My heart suddenly pounding.

Fuck. She came.

I stride into the house and open the door.

'Hi,' she says.

Oh, Tasha, Tasha, Tasha.

I pull her in, kick the door shut and, taking her in my arms, crush her mouth with mine and kiss the shit out of her. She melts against my body. While I kiss her my hands are undressing her. Her sweater, her top, her bra, her jeans, her underwear. Suddenly I see them. I grab her wrist and bring it up.

'He did this?' I ask, my voice deceptively soft.

She shakes her head and I feel her trembling. 'It's nothing. I bruise easily.'

Fury like I have never experienced slams into my gut. I can't even think straight with it. How fucking dare he? Who the fuck does that pompous sack of shit think he is? I won't, I can't take this lying down. 'I'll kill the fucking cunt.'

She puts her palms on either side of my face, her eyes suddenly brimming with tears. 'Don't. Don't spoil tonight. Who knows what tomorrow will bring.'

I look at the sad desperation in her face, and even though it makes me sick to my stomach, I control myself. For now. Taking deep breaths, I calm myself, but fucking hell, he has made himself an unforgiving nemesis.

'Tell me exactly what happened,' I demand.

She bows her head. 'It doesn't matter.'

'If you don't tell me I'll get it directly from him, and it won't be pretty,' I warn, my voice cold and quiet.

Her head flies up. 'No, don't,' she cries.

I stare hard at her. She seems suddenly so pale and vulnerable I want to hold her tightly and never let her leave this house. I soften my voice. 'Then tell me,' I coax.

'You shouldn't have bought the earrings. You shouldn't have showed your hand. It was a rash thing to do. Now he knows that you and I are ...' She shudders. 'What if he tells my father?'

I don't tell her that I wanted to show my hand. I wanted to rattle his cage. I'm not going to stand for her having to sneak around in the middle of the night to see me. I want to blow it all out of the water. I want to stand in front of her father come what may. War or not, I'll declare that she is mine.

I bring her wrist to my mouth and kiss the blue marks his fingers have left on her skin. Her expression is troubled, and it kills me that I can't erase that look of fear and worry or protect her. That tomorrow at dawn I will again have let her go. And while she is out of my sight anything could happen to her. Oh, God, even the thought of anything happening to her. I pull her soft body against mine and breathe in the clean, sweet smell.

'I'm sorry I couldn't protect you from that sick coward,' I mutter into her soft hair.

'It's okay. It's not your responsibility.'

That is where she is wrong. She *is* my responsibility. Every inch of skin on her body is my responsibility.

'I'm here now, so what're you going to do about it, mmm?'

I feel her body wriggle and rub wantonly against mine and immediately the uncontrollable lust she always invokes in my loins overtakes me.

I pull away slightly, cup her bare breasts, and let my thumbs caress the stiff peaks. I can't help being sinfully aroused by the startling contrast of my darker skin against her white flesh.

There is a condom in my trouser pocket and I fish it out. While I gently chew her nipples she groans hoarsely. I unzip my pants and release my straining cock. I push her up against the wall, stabbing my tongue into her open mouth and my cock into her pussy at the same time.

I plunder her mouth while my hands grab the firm cheeks of her ass and pull her even tighter against my cock. Wild and unashamed she sucks my tongue and rocks her hips into me. I release her mouth to return to her breasts. I want to see them twice their size, as they were last night. I draw the tips into my mouth and suck them roughly. Her cheeks are flushed and her eyes are glazed with passion. She furrows her fingers into my hair and presses my head closer to her body.

'Yes, yes,' she almost sobs with pleasure.

I nip one of the buds and she gasps. The sound touches something dark and forbidden inside me. I bend down to pick her up then stride to the living room. I put her down in the middle of the room and take a step back.

Let me see if she understands what I want from her.

Nineteen

Tasha Evanoff

https://www.youtube.com/watch?v=x_f5 6CZ99JY
What A Feeling

Breathing heavily, he stares down at me. The contrast between the snowy white dress shirt and his deep tan makes his face look predatory and fierce. He starts to undo his cufflinks. Dropping them to the floor he unbuttons his shirt.

His face is unsmiling and watchful.

For a second I don't understand, and then I do, and a thrill of excitement runs through me. I smile a little secret smile before I turn around and walk away from him. Four steps into the room and I slowly twirl back, sink to my knees, and assume the position. My head bowed, my knees well apart, my bottom on the backs of my heels, and my hands spread out on my thighs close to my knees. Complete submission.

I hear the rustle of his shirt and pants falling to the floor, the thud of his shoes hitting the ground. He comes forward and circles me.

'Look at me, Tasha,' he orders.

I obey.

He puts his hand on my bare shoulder and strokes it. 'You are mine.'

'I know.'

'From the moment your eyes met mine that summer by the pool you've been mine, and you'll always be mine.'

I rise to my knees and remain rock still, my mouth frozen open in front of him. He takes the condom off and his cock is dripping copious amounts of pre-cum. He moves closer to me, but not close enough that I don't have to lean forward to an almost precarious angle to snake my tongue out and run it slowly up the side of his shaft and over his cockhead.

He is so warm, his scent intoxicating. *This is my man*, I think with dizzy pleasure.

He intertwines his fingers into my hair and plunges his entire shaft deep into my throat making me gag, and saliva floods my mouth. He withdraws temporarily from the tightness of my throat. Then, taking advantage of the extra lubrication of my saliva, he pulls my head as close as possible to him and fucks my mouth.

'You've had this coming to you for a long time,' he groans. 'You deliberately teased me with your delicious body from the first moment you laid eyes on me, didn't you?'

My mouth stuffed with hard cock, I nod, making my head bob.

'You've given me a fucking hard-on for years. Now you have to pay for that.'

I nod.

'Tell me,' he commanded, 'that none of the fools you've known has ever fucked you like this.'

I give a shake to my head.

He pulls out of me. 'Say it,' he presses.

'No one has even come close to this.'

He smiles with satisfaction and saws deeper into my mouth. It doesn't take long before he explodes, filling my throat with hot cum. He looks down at me.

'Now go lie on the couch and spread your legs wide for me.' His smile is pure evil, and I shiver with anticipation.

I rise up and do as he asks, stretching myself over the couch so my legs are splayed open and my weeping center is exposed to his eyes. His eyes are hot wells of black tar as he approaches me.

He kneels between my legs and uses his thumbs to pull apart my pussy lips, then repeatedly licks at throbbing flesh as I gasp. His fingers dip into my slick entrance as his tongue rasps at my clit, lashing and stroking it until wild, high-pitched cries and shrieks stream from my mouth.

I rock my groin helplessly against his mouth and tongue as he continues to devour me. I can't even imagine what I must look like to him, naked, splayed wide open, and shamelessly begging for more, while he sucks my bud and fucks me with his fingers.

He switches his fingers for his thumb, which he slowly rubs inside me, up and down until my skin grows hot and my hips are lifting off the couch. Then he thrusts his thumb into me harder and rougher. My body tightens unbearably as the tension ratchets higher. I hear myself moaning and pleading with him not to stop as he continues to stab into me. At this point though, things are so heated, he is fucking me as hard as I am fucking his thumb.

His greedy tongue laves across my spread labia from top to bottom. I never imagined any man could be so committed to the enjoyment of my flesh. He devours me until I begin to shake and my fingers dig into his shoulder. Finally, I go rigid as the tension peaks. It holds me in its thrall before crashing over me in an earth-shattering roar. While I ride out the storm, Noah continues to use his fingers and mouth. He doesn't stop, even after uncontrollable hot juices gush out of me and all over his thumb and mouth. My head rolls back.

Oh my God! Have I just peed on him?

Flushed, dazed, horribly embarrassed, and unable to move, I look into his eyes. As I try to recover, I realize how hard and horny he is just from watching me, and how much he needs to come again. He doesn't try to take me. He just smiles softly and gathers me in his arms. 'Oh, look at you,' he croons. 'You're just a baby.'

'I'm sorry,' I croak.

He jerks his head back in surprise. 'For what?'

'You know why,' I mutter, too embarrassed to even say the words.

'Actually, I don't.'

'I peed on you.'

He chuckles. 'You didn't pee on me. I stimulated your G-spot so you squirted for me and that was beautiful to watch.'

He kisses me on my mouth. Gently. Sweetly. Protectively. It is the safest feeling in his arms. I forget Oliver and his threats, and my father with his insect eyes.

There is a sudden flash of light in the room then a rumble of thunder.

'The storm is here,' I whisper. 'I've always loved watching storms. Even when I was a little girl.'

He smiles at me. 'Want to watch it in the next room while we eat?'

My first reaction is to refuse food.

'I have *Chak-Chak*,' he says with a wickedly impish grin.

Oh, deep fried little logs of unleavened dough topped with hot honey

135

syrup. It's been a long time since I had some. Come to think of it, I was wound up at the dinner and hardly ate any of it. 'In that case, okay,' I agree with a happy grin.

'I'm going to have a bowl of *zharkoye* too. Want one?' he offers.

'Who made it?'

'Irina brought it in this morning. She makes it at her home.'

Homemade beef stew. The ultimate in comfort food and a definite must when watching a storm outside. 'All right,' I concur, 'but only a little for me.'

He uncurls himself and pulls me up with him.

'Are you cold? Do you want something to wear?' he asks.

'I'll wear your shirt,' I say, going to his discarded shirt and slipping my arms through the oversized sleeves. It smells of him and I hug it close to my body.

Noah rolls up the shag carpet and slings it over one shoulder. We go through to the next reception room. Glass doors open out to the garden. Noah unrolls the carpet in front of the doors. Taking the cushions from the couches, he throws them on the carpet.

'Do you want some blankets?'

'No, I'm not cold,' I reply.

'Fine. Wait here for me,' he says, and goes out of the door.

Twenty

Tasha Evanoff

I lie back propped up against cushions on the shag carpet and look at the black sky as it streaks with flashes of white lightning. The power of it leaves me strangely excited. I count the seconds before the thunderclaps. One, two, three. Hmm ... using the counting system of Baba, where one second is equivalent to one mile, the storm is only three miles away. It could get to where we are. The storm could break over us ... if we are lucky.

In minutes Noah is back carrying a tray. Two steaming bowls of stew and a plate piled high with Chak-Chak. I dip my spoon into the rich brown liquid and put a bit of potato and beef into my mouth. The meat is so tender it disintegrates on my tongue.

'Mmmm ... Irina is really good,' I say. I close my eyes. 'I can taste the cloves and the dill, but she's also used another ingredient.' I pause and frown. 'I think it's rosemary. No, wait. It's not. It's actually oregano,' I decide finally.

He looks at me with an odd smile.

'What?'

'You remind me of a joke my restaurant manager once told me.'

'Go on then, share it. I can see you're dying to tell me.' I put a mouthful of food into my mouth and look at him expectantly.

He grins. 'There was this gourmet who had an amazing sense of smell. He was very proud of it because it was so damn accurate and strong. All he had to do was smell a fork or a knife and he could tell exactly what food had been eaten using that utensil. He could do this even after it had been washed. Every time he went to the restaurant he wouldn't let the waiter or waitress show him the menu, or tell him the special. He would simply smell the fork and know every single dish that the restaurant specialized in.

'One day he goes into this Italian restaurant and, as usual, before the waiter can tell him the specials for the night, he holds up his hand. "Let me see if I can guess," he says.

'The waiter looks at him strangely, thinking, Oh God, I'm getting too old for this job. Silently he gestures for the man to proceed. The man smells the fork. "Ah," he says. "You have sea bass baked with anchovies and olives, but the Chef has put a touch too much lemon juice in that dish so I won't have that. Instead I'll have the chicken with Parma ham, and the baked potato which also smells good."

'Shocked, the waiter asks, "You got all that from smelling the fork?"

'The man explains about his amazing sense of smell but, of course, the old waiter suspects it must be a trick. He must know someone who has been in that restaurant before. However, he wants his tip so he quietly serves the man's meal to him. For dessert the waiter opens his mouth to tell him the specials. Again the man puts out his hand and smells the spoon. "Ah, it seems as if the Tiramisu is very fresh."

'Now the waiter is convinced someone is playing a trick on him. "Yes, Sir, the tiramisu was made this morning," he says politely. "Yes, I will have that then," says the man.

'The waiter resolves to play a little trick of his own on the man. "No, no, before you make your decision there is a very special dish that the Chef has prepared that has not yet been served to anyone else. I will let you smell it and guess for yourself. And if you correctly guess it you can have your entire meal on the house."

'The man agrees.

'The waiter goes into the kitchen to the back where Maria is working washing dishes. He gives her an unused plastic spoon. "Listen, Maria, can you do me a favor and rub this quickly between your legs?"

'Maria is a simple girl. "Okay," she agrees and she sticks the spoon into her panties.

'The waiter washes the spoon, then wipes it down carefully, and carries it to the man.

'The man brings the spoon to his nose and sniffs it. He sniffs it once, then twice. Looking perplexed, he turns to the waiter. "But, Maria works here too?" he asks.'

I burst out laughing. 'That's a good one.'

He laughs too and suddenly I feel really close to him. As if we have been together for years and years.

'So tell me about you?' I ask, putting the empty bowl down.

'What do you want to know?'

'Why would a man like you join the Mafia?'

His face closes over. He shrugs. 'I had my reasons.'

I rise to my knees and, leaning over, kiss him on his eyelids. 'Tell me. Let me in,' I plead.

He lays his cheek on my breast. 'I needed money, a lot of it, and quickly,' he says.

'Why?' I whisper.

'I was fifteen and my mother was ill. I didn't know how else to get it.'

'What about your father?'

'My father disappeared after he had impregnated my mother.'

'Oh, Noah,' I sigh. In my mind's eye I could see him, a tall, lanky boy, whipcord lean, his eyes anxious. 'What happened?'

'Yeah, I got the money, but she passed away in less than two months. I tried to get out of the brotherhood by paying the debt back, but of course they didn't want the money. Less than £20,000 for a soul is a bargain.'

'I'm so sorry.'

He shakes his head. 'For two months she was comfortable. I would do it all again if I had to,' he says fiercely.

'I'm sorry you were forced into this terrible life.'

'It wasn't terrible to start with. I was just a thief, but this job slowly seeps into every crack and crevice of your life. It takes more and more of you until it becomes you and you become it. You are a thief, a counterfeiter, an enforcer, a murderer.'

'So how did you come to England?'

'I was on a job and I met Alexander Malenkov. He was called Zane then. He was leaving Russia for England. I had nothing left in the motherland. Babushka had just passed away that year so I followed him. We worked well together and we formed our own thing.'

He picks up the plate of Chak-Chak and offers it to me. I take one.

'We were Mafia, but we only specialized in the finance industry. We targeted banks and large financial organizations. We were stealing from the biggest crooks of all time. It felt good.'

I chew the Chak-Chak and swallow it.

'Occasionally we were forced to do business with your father or people like him, but as much as possible we kept away from organized crime outside of our small but loyal group. Then a couple of years ago Alexander met Dahlia and she persuaded him to follow his true talent and become the pianist he is now. By then I had saved a lot of money from our dealings together so I bought all his clubs and restaurants. And here we are.'

Outside the first fat drops of rain fall. They become a torrent quickly. I turn towards him. 'Isn't it beautiful? It's like there is no one else in the world except us in this house.'

He stares at me.

'Shall we go out in it?' I ask.

His eyebrows fly upwards. 'You want to play in the rain?' he asks incredulously.

'Yeah.'

'It's autumn rain. It'll be cold.'

'So what? We're Russian. The cold doesn't bother us.'

'It was you I was thinking of.'

'I love the rain.'

He stands and opens the door. Fresh air hits us. He is naked and I am only wearing his shirt. I take his hand and we go out onto the springy wet grass. Indeed, the rain *is* cold and we are quickly drenched, but we both laugh like children.

'Will you dance with me?' I shout above the noise of the pouring rain.

'It might not be—'

'When a lady asks you to dance with her, you dance with her,' I mock sternly.

'Don't take that tone with me young lady.'

'Or what?' I challenge.

'Or this.' He slams me against his body and kisses me passionately. Water runs down our fused bodies. It's beautiful. And ... I will never forget this moment.

Afterwards, we go back inside, dry ourselves, and he makes love to me on the shag carpet. Outside the rain pours and lightning flashes across the sky. I will never forget this night.

Twenty-one

Tasha Evanoff

https://www.youtube.com/watch?v=yWeg-Woxyok
I Got It

Yay! Papa is away!

It is the third day of him going away and Noah and I are on a day trip to Nice. Blue seas, blue skies, and gorgeous sunshine. The car Noah hired is an open-top, green BMW, and the wind rushes into my hair as we coast along the Promenade des Anglais.

Wintering British nobles of the 19th century who came here to escape the dreary English weather set the snooty tone by paving a marble walkway to run alongside the beach. It goes all the way from the airport to right into the city. We pass people rollerblading on it as we drive along. The sight fills me with a happy, carefree buzz. Nowhere else in the world can you rollerblade from the beach all the way to the airport if you so desire.

I hold my hair plastered to the sides of my face and direct a face-splitting grin at Noah. The wind has pushed his hair away from his, making his cheekbones look cut and chiseled. I stare at him. He looks like a movie star, a god, an angel, or something impossibly gorgeous.

'What?'

'Nothing,' I say, still grinning uncontrollably. I've never been this happy in my life before.

He smiles back.

I turn away and gaze contentedly at the blue-green ocean. I have never been to the French Riviera before, and this one-day break with Noah is just pure magic.

Actually, it has been pretty magical ever since Papa left.

I've spent every wonderful, lust-filled night with Noah. I also bought a pay-as-you-go cellphone, and the sensation of having him at the other end of my phone at any time of the day is simply exhilarating. It is like we are truly boyfriend and girlfriend. On the second

day I even took Sergei out to the park to meet him. Yeah, Sergei completely adored Noah.

'Meet my son, Sergei.'

Noah smiled. 'He's as gorgeous as his mother.'

'Shake hands, Sergei,' I told my boy, and beamed proudly when he lifted his paw to be shaken by Noah.

'He's well trained,' Noah noted, impressed.

Proudly, I told him that I never trained Sergei. In fact, when he was a small puppy he was the naughtiest, wildest devil you ever saw. He was just terrible. I would come into my bathroom to find that he had shredded the toilet paper to bits. The whole bathroom floor was covered in it, and he'd be sitting there with an expression that said, so what are you going to do about it? Nothing was safe from him. He would come to me with something he shouldn't have in his mouth and challenge me to chase him for it.

Everybody told me I was spoiling him. I shouldn't let him sleep with me. I should cage him. I should send him to obedience classes. I was ruining him, but

I refused, because I didn't want him to feel that he was my little slave. Sit, stand, or roll over when I told him to. To me he was my baby. Besides, every time I went to scold him, he would look at me with his great big puppy dog eyes and I would melt.

He was my heart and I loved him.

When he broke Baba's glasses, Papa was furious, but I had no concern other than he might end up swallowing a fragment of glass. He remained a thorn in all the servants' sides until he was about a year old. Then he slowly started to change. He grew up. He became so good I didn't even need a lead to take him out. He knew what made me happy and he immediately did that. We were so bonded, words were not necessary. He instinctively knew if a man coming towards me had bad intentions, and he'd growl and bare his teeth until the man backed off.

Noah laughed. 'A dog after my own heart.'

Afterwards, we bought hotdogs. Sergei had his with no mustard, I had mine with just one line, and Noah very bravely had two.

'That's where the kick comes from,' he said wolfing it all down easily.

In the evenings we went to restaurants outside London and we behaved as if we were just another ordinary couple having a night out. No bodyguards, drivers, or fear of anything. We fed each other little bits of food, we laughed, and we hired rooms in little-known countryside hotels. We spent all night having wild sex then, wrapped up in each other's arms, we talked the rest of the night away. Well, I did most of the talking. He's not much of a talker.

And now here we are in Nice.

The lazy October sunshine is deliciously yellow and warm. The architecture and buildings are so Mediterranean and baroque you could be forgiven for thinking you are in Italy. Nice is also the place some of the best Russians families came to so they needed a house of worship that was worthy of their status. Hence, Nice boasts one of the finest Russian orthodox churches outside of Russia. Baba has asked me to pay a visit to it and light a candle for Papa.

'Can we go to the church? I promised my grandmother that I would light a candle.'

'Sure,' Noah agrees easily, 'but first breakfast.'

Breakfast is *socca* at a stall in the Cours Saleya market in the colorful old town. It is brought piping hot in the back of a scooter by a man. Turns out it is a traditional peasant snack and is basically a very large chick pea pancake with a lots of pepper. It is served on paper with no cutlery, and is surprisingly delicious served with a glass of local rosé.

Feeling pleasantly tipsy after the one and a half glasses of rosé so early in the morning, I lean into Noah's hardness as we pass by a myriad of sounds and sights. We walk together, our bodies sometimes touching on the vehicle-free streets. The sun beats down on my head and I can taste the salty air on my lips. In the butcher's window I see a tiny whole dead piglet tied up with string.

'Oh my God. Look! Why would anyone keep something so gruesome in the window?' I exclaim with surprise.

'That's *prochetta*. An Italian style specialty. It's actually a hollowed-out pig filled with chunks of meat, fat, herbs, and lots of garlic before being roasted on a spit. They slice right through it and serve it in large thin slices as you would lunch meat.

'Ugh. Food with faces. Just no.'

'It's actually very delicious,' he tells me.

'Why did you buy a house here?' I ask him nosily.

He shrugs. 'The weather is pleasant and I like that there is a big Russian community here.'

'Do you speak French?'

'Nope. I get by with English and Russian. Do you?'

'I studied it at school, but I'm rusty.'

'Good, you can do all the speaking from now on,' he says.

'Tell me, what were you were like as a child?' I press. Left to his own devices, he says very little. I want to know everything there is to know about him.

He gives my question some thought as if no one had ever asked him such a question before. 'Serious. Eager to please. Loyal, very loyal. And you?'

There it is again. Turning the conversation back to me. I look at him behind my eyelashes. Never mind, he cannot hide forever. Little by little I will teach him to trust me and reveal himself to me.

'I was a plump, terrible, little thing. In the summer months I lay on the cool floor totally naked and refused to get dressed, and in the winter I ran around looking for places to hide so I could jump out with a great roar and frighten my mother and Baba.'

He laughs.

I smile. 'Yup, I did that. They would pretend to scream and I thought that was hilarious, and I would fall about laughing. I mean, I would be clutching my stomach and rolling on the ground.'

'I would have liked to have seen that,' he says, smiling. 'I'll have to get you to hide in one of my cupboards.'

'It won't work. I lost the ability to laugh like that. Now I find it almost impossible to laugh uncontrollably.'

He stares into my eyes. 'I never laughed like that even when I was a child.'

'Why?'

'Probably because my mother was always so sad. She never got over being discarded by my father.'

'Do you ever miss Russia?' I ask softly.

'No.'

'No?'

He shakes his head. 'When I was younger I used to dream of my childhood days. I could even remember taking my first steps holding on to my mother's finger. The memories came so close I could feel them breathing into my mouth, but there is nothing left of them now. The house, the people, the memories. They're all gone ... I don't think of them anymore.'

Twenty-two

Tasha Evanoff

The church is located in a green area of the city, and you cannot see it until you are actually almost upon it. It has six onion domes and an exterior that is richly decorated in mosaic. Add those features to the fact that it is nearly hidden makes it seem foreign, isolated, almost an oasis in that bustling city.

There is a guard at the door, a man in all black. Even his glasses have black frames. He has a dour totally Russian personality, but strangely, he doesn't speak Russian. He speaks to us first in French then in English. He is apparently there to enforce the rules. Basically, no taking pictures or videos. No talking loudly. No shorts. No naked shoulders.

I brought a scarf with me and use it to cover my hair before we enter the church. The interior is even more grand and fabulous than the exterior. There are no chairs, but it is very much a working church attended by the large Russian community that live in Nice. In the Orthodox Church the congregation stands.

It is full of stunningly beautiful and intricate icons and paintings. Hundreds of candles burn, adding to the hushed, otherworldly atmosphere. Religious artifacts include a huge hammered silver cross, and delicate icons made of silver and studded with semi-precious stones.

'I have to light a candle for Papa,' I whisper into the solemn air.

He looks at me strangely. 'My grandmother asked me to,' I explain with a shrug.

He waits for me while I go up to the icon of a saint. Bowing my head in veneration, I say a prayer for Papa. 'Please make Papa repent. Enter his heart.' Then I look deep into the icon's eyes because Baba says that if you do this while meditating, you will enter a lake where you will meet your own soul. Of course, I have never prayed long enough for that to happen, and it does not happen now either.

Pulling a tissue out of my purse, I wipe my lipstick off before I kiss the icon on the hand as a sign of love and faith. We never kiss the faces of icons as Judas betrayed Christ with a kiss on the cheek. I light my candle and plant it before stepping away, then make the sign of the cross over my face before going to join Noah.

'You love your father,' he says, almost to himself, as we leave the cool exterior of the church and come out into the sunshine again.

I stop and look up at him. He seems surprised that I would, and I can understand why he would be. He needs to know how I feel.

'I know Papa has done some really bad things to my mother. When I was small I saw him push my mother to the front door and kick her so viciously she flew out the door and fell sprawled on the front steps. In one instant all those years with her came to that. I wouldn't do that to a stray dog. He treated her like she was nothing. While she was still standing there bleeding, crying, and screaming that he was wrong, she had not been unfaithful to him, he closed the door on her and forbade me to ever see her again.'

Noah stares at me, shocked.

'The thing is, my mother hadn't been disloyal to him. You have to be a very brave fool indeed to be unfaithful to my father.'

Noah's eyes widen. 'And that was the last you saw of your mother?'

I shook my head. 'No. My grandmother made sure I saw her regularly when my father was away. I still do. Secretly.'

'Good,' he mutters softly.

'When I was young I used to dream of a father who loved me, took me out to eat ice cream, or watch a movie with me, but my father is not like that, and I've learned to live with it.' I smile. 'It's better to have a father than to have none at all. He's the only father I have, maybe I do love him. In his own cold way Papa loves me too.'

He tilts his head and looks at me as if I am a creature he doesn't understand. 'Doesn't it bother you though that he is forcing you to marry a man you don't love?'

'He's not forcing me to marry Oliver. He ... suggested it and I agreed.'

'Really? You had a choice?'

I bite my lower lip. 'When I agreed to marry Oliver I had no one and it didn't seem like a bad thing. He was from a good family and he was easy on the eye. I had met him a few times and he was always courteous and solicitous. However, I recently found out something about Oliver. He's not what he seems to be. I think he may be into perverted things. I know Papa has ambitions, but he wants me to be happy too, and I could never be happy with such a man. When Papa comes back I'm going to tell him that in these circumstances I cannot marry Oliver.'

To my surprise Noah doesn't make any comment at all. Instead he veils his eyes so I won't be able to tell what he is thinking. 'I thought we could try some parasailing before lunch,' he says, completely changing the subject.

'Parasailing? I'm game,' I say immediately.

We make our way to the water sports center on the Promenade des Anglais, and I see the yellow parachutes with their distinctive yellow smiley faces floating in the hot blue sky over the sea. Noah has already booked a slot for us and he hands our vouchers over.

An instructor with a bronze tan and strong French accent gives us a safety briefing and a lesson on parasailing basics. Then I step into a safety harness together with Noah. We wade out into the warm water. Our instructor connects our harness to the giant parasail and a pull rope attached to a speed boat. The boat pulls forward, our sail fills with air, and we rise into the sky.

'Oh, my God. We're airborne. We're flying,' I scream as we soar up more than a hundred meters into the sky. The wind rushes into my face and it is the most thrilling sensation to be so high up. Giddy with excitement, I whoop like a child when we rise even higher.

'Whoopeee ... check out how far we are from the ground,' I shriek, pointing to our small shadows on the sea's surface.

Noah just chuckles at my enthusiasm.

As we glide effortlessly over the Baie des Anges, we enjoy stunning aerial views of the French Riviera's sandy coastline, the turquoise blue waters of the Mediterranean, the rolling hills of Provence, and Nice's historic streets. As the boat makes its turn we drift back down for a water landing as the boat slowly comes to a stop.

'Oh my God, we are going to crash land,' I scream again. Splash. Oops. Ha, ha.

'You smell of the sea,' Noah says with a laugh, as he catches me and holds me close to him.

High from the unforgettable experience, I throw my arms around his neck. 'That was wonderful, Noah. I loved it. Can we go again?'

'If you enjoyed this you must come paragliding with me. It's even better. You are not towed by a boat but driven by the sheer force of the wind, and you race through the sky.'

'Is that your hobby then?'

We start to wade back to shore. 'I don't know if it is a hobby, but I like it.'

'Do you paraglide in England?' I enquire.

'Usually in Nepal, the desert, or where there are mountains.'

We are standing in the water, the waves sucking at our feet. 'Maybe you'll take me with you one day,' I hear myself say.

Twenty-three

Tasha Evanoff

https://www.youtube.com/watch?v=LX
HzZBr_zuU
The Last Unicorn

We have lunch by the beach. Salad Nicoise, fresh pasta with pesto, and hollowed out fruit and vegetables stuffed with meat. We are both ravenous after the parasailing, and we polish our plates off in quick time.

'What's next on the itinerary?' I ask, putting my fork and knife down.

'You choose. Henri Matisse or Marc Chagall museum,' he says, wiping his mouth.

'Marc Chagall,' I say immediately, beaming at him. 'He's actually my favorite artist.'

'How patriotic of you.'

I shake my head earnestly. 'The fact that he was Russian has got nothing to do with it. He was a genius. I totally agree with Picasso who said, "The man must have an angel in his head."'

He smiles at my enthusiasm.

'Don't you like him?' I ask curiously.

One of his shoulders lifts and falls. 'I've never really studied fine art appreciation, or had a chance to know much about it. My life took me on a different path. Tattoos is the closest I've come to art.'

'You introduced me to parasailing. I'll introduce you to Chagall,' I say excitedly. 'Looking at his paintings is like gazing into a magical world. He makes you want to believe in unicorns.'

'Well then, to Chagall's world we go.' A masculine grin that I usually associate with tanned, devil-may-care cowboys plays on his lips.

I lean my chin on my hand. 'Noah?'

'Yeah.'

'Thank you for bringing me on this trip. I've really enjoyed it. I can't think of a time I've been happier in my life.'

Something flashes in his eyes, then it is gone. It is so quick I can't tell whether he is embarrassed, amused, or something else completely different.

⁂

The museum is on a hill in a very quiet area compared to the hustle and bustle of the city we have come from. We pay our ten euros and enter. The walls of the hexagon shaped spaces are stark white, making the large paintings pop.

While we sit on the wooden benches and gaze at Chagall's masterpieces, all at once generous, naive, shrewd, secretive, sad, vulnerable and full of love and joy, I tell Noah little interesting tit bits I have gleaned about the painter over the years.

'Do you know he was so poor he used to eat the head of a mackerel one day and save the tail for another? Then when he met the woman he would marry she would knock on his window to bring him cakes and milk. Later he said of her, "I only had to open the window of my room and blue air, love and flowers entered with her."' I pause to look at Noah. 'Isn't that the most romantic thing you ever heard?'

'No,' he says. 'The most romantic thing I ever heard of was when a beautiful blonde came into my office for a night of lust wearing a pink cardigan.'

I giggle softly. 'It was that or the see-through dress with the plunging neckline.'

'I'm glad the pink cardigan won the day.'

'Why? Wouldn't you have preferred me in the see-through?'

'No. I wouldn't change a thing from that night.'

When we stand in front of a photograph of Chagall with his mischievous faun-like face and strange, almond-shaped eyes, I turn to Noah and ask, 'Do you know he prepared his charcoal pencils, holding them in his hand like a little bouquet?'

Noah gazes at me as if he is looking at something he has always wanted, but never thought he could have.

'Holding them so he would sit in front of a blank canvas and wait for an idea to come. When it came, he raised the charcoal and very quickly started tracing straight lines, ovals, lozenges. Out of those shapes, as if by magic, a clown would appear, then a unicorn, a violinist, a pilgrim, an angel. Once the outline was done he would step back and sit down again, as exhausted as a boxer after a round. Imagine how his mind must have been. The whole picture was clear to him in one flash of inspiration.'

'That's an amazing talent to have,' Noah says slowly.

'Yes, it must be wonderful to have such a unique ability. He once confessed that all he wanted to do was to stay wild and untamed ... to shout, weep, pray.'

Twenty-four

Tasha Evanoff

Our next stop is Cap de Nice, where Noah's house is. It is set high on the hill. He opens the tall door and we enter an elegant art deco villa full of natural light. We go through the living room with its impressive chandelier made of capiz shells. When he opens the sliding doors, the mother-of-pearl discs twinkle in the strong wind that rushes in.

I move closer to the doors and see that the house is built on rocky ground. It has a hundred-and-eighty-degree view of the sea front and boasts several terraces and balconies.

'Wow, this is amazing,' I say.

'I know,' he says softly. 'It's the reason I bought this house.'

I step out onto the terrace and see the steps cut into the jagged white rocks. One set diverts off towards a white stone platform where you can stand and look out at the breathtaking view of the ocean, and the other offshoot leads down to a small private beach.

He takes my hand and leads me out of the shade of the terrace towards the steps. The sun is beating down on them making them glare with heat and light.

I shade my eyes with my hand. 'I can't stay long in the sun. I don't want to get a tan. It will be a dead giveaway that I've been out of the country.'

'Don't worry. I won't keep you out here for long,' he says, stripping off. Naked and staring into my eyes, he unzips my dress and lets it drop to the ground. Underneath I am wearing my green and blue bikini. He pulls me onto the burning tiles of the terrace.

'Are we going to have sex on the beach?' I ask with a grin.

'Not on the beach. Think of all that sand in all the wrong places.'

'Ouch.'

'I want to take you at the water's edge.'

I look around. We are not actually alone. In the distance there are figures. 'People can see us,' I protest.

'I don't care,' he says, leading me to the water's edge. 'I want you right now.' He pushes me so that I overbalance and we topple onto the damp sand. It feels lovely and cool against my bare skin. His stomach and legs are hot and smooth on my belly and thighs. The sand gives as I wriggle underneath him. He pins my wrists above my head.

'Trapped,' he growls.

'And loving it,' I whisper.

He unclasps my bikini top and flings it away. The sun beats down on my exposed breasts. The sensation is just delicious. My nipples harden with the look in his eyes. A wave comes up high enough to tickle my toes.

'Surely there must be some law that makes this indecent exposure or illegal,' I gasp.

'We're in Europe. On a private beach. No one gives a shit,' he mutters, his eyes hot and dark with lust. He kisses my breasts and I close my eyes and enjoy the pleasurable sensation. He sucks my nipples until they harden almost painfully.

Another wave teaming with bubbles hits us, I barely feel it. All my attention is focused on him pushing aside my bikini bottom. Then he is suddenly inside me, big, hard and strong. He swallows the small startled cry that races out of my mouth in a fierce kiss, and only breaks it to stare deeply into my eyes. His black eyes are pits of shifting emotion as he moves steadily inside me.

The waves lap between and around our bodies, coming right up to my waist. He pulls out of me.

'Turn around and show me your pussy,' he orders.

'What, here?'

'Uh-huh.'

I turn my head. The figures are still on the beach, but they're too far away to see my face and they probably can't see what we're up to, and if they can, so what, I'll never see them again in my life.

I turn onto my elbows and knees, my breasts dangling and dragging in the wet sand. He pulls my bikini bottom down my thighs to expose my sex. Bracing his hands on my hips, he shoves his cock into me. My whole body spasms, my toes curl into the sand, my back arches, and a soft scream exits my mouth. A wave breaks and runs under me, washing my nipples with silky warm water. Sand slips underneath me. The surf swells up over my calves as he plunges again and again.

I look up and see the bright blue sky. What if one of the figures comes down the beach? Discovery is a thrilling thought. A bigger wave sweeps over my body, belly and breasts. I look down between my knees and at Noah's sturdy masculine legs as he pumps steadily into me.

He reaches with his hand and circles my clit. My breathing becomes uneven. Soon my climax will be upon me. He thrusts harder and faster, pushing me deeper into the sand. I lift my head towards the sky and wait for it. It rushes in as a large wave crashes into me, soaking my body, soaking my sex, submerging my hands. I feel the suction of the water as the wave returns to the ocean. I feel my body float like a piece of driftwood, if not for Noah's firm grip. I begin to tense, my whole body stiffening. I shiver. With a roar he withdraws, and I feel his hot cum shooting onto my back as I go over the edge.

He pulls my bikini bottom back up and splashes my back with seawater. Then we scramble further up the shore and collapse on the dry, hot sand. We watch the sunset filling the sky with russets and pinks, and when I turn to look at his face it is lit with the same colors. My heart trembles with love. I touch his cheek with my fingertips and he smiles.

'You look beautiful in this light,' he purrs.

'Funny, I was thinking the same thing,' I say, and his lips crash down on mine. I hear a soft moan escape my lips.

For dinner he takes me to *La Merenda*. It's a quirky, tiny, crowded place where everybody sits on stools with their shoulders and elbows practically rubbing. Wine is effectively red or white out of juice glasses. Don't even mention the word Coke! They don't take credit cards and you can't even call to reserve a table. Noah sent someone to go there physically the day before to book us a table.

You sit at the table and watch Dominic La Stanc, a world renowned chef, who used to work for the most expensive restaurant in Nice, perform a smooth ballet with his sous chef and the *one* waiter tasked with serving all twenty-four tables in the restaurant. They have a small, traditional menu written in chalk on a blackboard, but when the food arrives it is clear why people are willing to put up with the inconveniences and discomfort.

I have the *fleur de courgette*, (the yellow zucchini blossom) battered and deep-fried to make a sort of flower fritter. It is a dream of a dish. For my second course I have the beef with orange and it absolutely sings. After a lemon tart baked to perfection, it is time to go back to London.

I must admit I left a part of my heart in France.

Twenty-five

Tasha Evanoff

One day before Papa comes home I arrange a meeting with Mama. We meet in our usual place — the ladies toilet in Harrods. A long time ago we decided that it was perfect for us. It is very clean and beautiful. It's more like the fine dressing room of a rich Russian or Arab woman. The staff never bother us, leaving us alone to chat quietly. When it is time for us to leave, usually thirty or forty minutes later, I slip a fifty pound note into their tip saucer. I don't know what Vadim must be thinking about my time in the toilet, but so far he has pretended it is normal for me to disappear into the toilet and come out nearly an hour later.

To avoid Vadim ever seeing my mother, she is already waiting in the toilet. I hug and kiss her and we sit down.

'You look wonderful. Have you been on the sunbed?' she asks.

'I've been to Nice,' I tell her.

She shakes her head. 'You didn't tell me you were going on holiday.'

'It was a surprise visit,' I tell her, smiling broadly.

Her face changes. 'What's going on, Tasha?'

I tell her about Noah. The whole time she frowns and looks more and more disturbed.

'Where is all of this going, Tasha?' she asks when I have told her everything.

'I love him, and I'm going to tell Papa when he gets back that I'm not going to marry Oliver.'

Her whole face contorts with fear. 'What?'

'I plan to tell Papa that I don't want to marry Oliver. I found out that Oliver is not what he has been pretending to be.'

'Oh, darling. That's not going to work with your father.'

'Why not?'

She shakes her head, her brow creased with anxiety. 'You don't know him like I do. He will not agree. His pride is at stake.'

'He will, Mama. I know he wants me to be happy. He thought I could be happy with Oliver, but once I tell him that I could never be happy he won't force me. Papa has never hurt me before.'

She looks at me pityingly. 'Oh, darling. You can never know your father. Until now you've never disobeyed him so you haven't seen anything but the face of a man who has everything going exactly the way he wants it. Have you ever wondered why he let you watch me being thrown out? Why should a child witness such a cruel and ugly scene?'

Yes, it bothered me for many years. I could never understand why he let me see it. To punish my mother? To show he was boss? 'Why?' I whisper.

'It was a warning to you. Disobey me and this is what I'm capable of.'

I feel her words like a chill on my skin, but I don't allow myself to absorb that idea. It is too frightening. I don't want to be dissuaded from my purpose.

'It'll be fine, Mama, you'll see. I'll convince Papa.'

Mama bows her head for a few seconds. When she raises her head, her eyes are troubled. 'Whatever you do, do not tell him about Noah.'

'I wasn't planning to,' I say quickly.

'Good. Just tell him you don't love Oliver and don't want to marry him because he is a pervert who will make you unhappy. Don't give him a focus for his anger, and do not be careless. After you tell your father, whatever method you are using to meet Noah, it would be wise to discard it and wait for the coast to completely clear before you attempt to see him again. Your father will immediately suspect that it is another man that has made you change your mind and he will be watching you closely.'

She looks sad.

'In fact,' she adds, 'I believe it may already be too late. You have most probably done something to alert him. Look at your face. You are glowing. I knew the moment I saw you that you were different.'

I lean forward, my heart beating fast. 'Do you really think he knows?'

'If I know him as well as I think I do, then, yes. He can read people like a book. He is waiting for you to make your next move so he can make his. He already knows his move.'

I feel a shiver of fear go through me. 'He loves me,' I insist stubbornly, because it is too painful for me to believe that my father could be such a bitter enemy of mine.

'Darling, darling Tasha. There is no other way to say this. Your father is a psychopath. Asking him to love you is like asking a plate or a table to love you. In fact, it would be unfair even to ask it of him because he can't do it. He is incapable of love. There is no one he truly loves other than himself. You and your Baba are around only because it suits him. If it didn't he would have no hesitation to get rid of either of you.'

I gasp.

'If you look deep into his eyes you will see nothing. There is nothing at his core. There is only a naked, all-consuming, aggressive, grotesque obsession for more and more and more material gain and glorification.'

That afternoon I go to see Baba. She is sitting in the garden with her coat and hat on, and her eyes are closed as she soaks in the last rays of the sun. She opens one eye when my shadow falls on her, before closing it back.

'Sit, Sergei,' I say as I sink into the chair next to hers. He lies down next to me.

'Baba,' I say, gently tickling Sergei behind his ear, and keeping my voice neutral and casual. 'Do you think that Papa loves me?'

She does a strange thing. She doesn't immediately look at me and say, of course, he does. She takes a deep breath and doesn't turn to look at me. 'Why do you ask this?'

'I don't know. I just wondered.'

'The honest answer is I don't know. Let's hope we never have to test his love for you.'

I chew at my bottom lip. 'Do you think this great alliance he has planned with Oliver is more important to him than my happiness?'

She sighs softly. 'I have always told you the truth, and no matter how much it hurts I will not lie to you. Your happiness is not more important than this alliance he has planned.'

'I see,' I note quietly. 'What will he do if I refuse to marry Oliver?'

She turns to me then, her eyes urgent. 'Do you really want your man?'

'Yes,' I say immediately.

'If you really value your dream, then you'll say nothing. You will give your father no warning, no opportunity to strike first. You will simply run away with your man. Take nothing that can be traced back to you. Leave every single person you know behind, and start again in South America, or Asia. Are you prepared to do that?'

'I can't leave you and Mama.'

'Then you will not have your dream,' she says with such finality that I grow cold inside.

I lean forward restlessly. 'But even if I could leave you and Mama, Noah will not consent to run and hide as if we have done something wrong, anyway. We'd be looking over our shoulders for the rest of our lives. Noah is not afraid of Papa. He says he is ready to take on Papa.'

In the last rays of the sun, Baba suddenly looks old. 'If what you say is true you must prepare for bloodshed. His or your father's.'

Twenty-six

Tasha Evanoff

https://www.youtube.com/watch?v=qT6XCvDUUsU
Why Does My Heart Feel So Bad?

Papa has come back home. It is incredible how quickly the time passed. When I kissed his cheeks and welcomed him back I felt a tremor of fear inside me.

Even now, as I stand outside his study, I am not ready to face him, but I will never be ready. Childishly, I wish I could turn back the clock even one day, but I cannot put off what has to be said. My hands shake as I take a deep breath to steel myself before I rap gently on his door.

'Who is it?' he asks.

'Tasha.'

'Come in.'

I let my hand drop to the door handle, turn it, and step into the room. My father is at his desk, his head bowed over some papers. He has his reading glasses on. He does not speak, just beckons me forwards with an open palm. I walk towards his desk, fear speeding through my body, and stand in front of him.

His dark, dead eyes peer over the rim of his glasses. 'Sit.'

'I prefer to stand, Papa.' My voice shakes. My father is a very intimidating man and it will be easier to keep my nerve if I am standing. Papa slumps back in his leather chair, removes his glasses, and lays them on the table.

'What do you want, Tasha?' His voice is totally expressionless and his face stony. I immediately feel unease. Mama was right. He is ready for me. He has been waiting for me to do this and he knows exactly what I am going to say.

I feel frozen with fear now, but I cannot turn back. I spit out the words I have rehearsed so many times. In the bed, in front of the mirror, in front of Baba.

'Papa, I'm sorry, but I cannot marry Oliver. I do not love him and I never will. I know that this is what you wanted, but this is my life and I deserve to choose who I marry.'

Papa smiles. It is a sly smile, and suddenly I know I should have listened to Baba. I should have persuaded Noah to run away with me. He would have done it for me, I know he would have. Instead, I have done exactly what Papa wanted, played right into his hands. How brilliantly he has played his game, and how silly I have been. Now he can execute his next move.

'This is not something I am asking of you, Tasha Evanoff,' he says gently.

Tears start running down my face. 'Papa, please don't ask me to do this. He is not the man you think he is. He has strange needs. He wants to do cruel things to me.'

'I know about his needs.' His voice is cold and hard. 'But he will not trouble you with them. I will make him understand on your wedding night that there are whores for such things. My daughter is to be treated like a Princess or she will be an early widow.'

I stare at him open-mouthed. 'Is that what you really want for me, Papa?'

The corners of his mouth turn downward. 'Is it so bad what I want for you? To be respected by society?' He shakes his head as if he can't understand me. 'When you marry Oliver you will become Lady Tasha. You will move into that splendid stately home and be the mistress of it. Your children will be Lords and Ladies. What does it matter if your husband visits a whore or two to satisfy his needs?'

'Oh, Papa, please. Please. I don't want to be Lady Tasha and I don't care if my kids are not Lords and Ladies. I want them to be happy. I want them to have a normal father and mother who love each other and love them too. I just want a small life with a husband I love and children that are happy and healthy.

'And I am telling you that you will marry Oliver Jarsdale. Do you understand?' he yells suddenly, slamming his fists onto his desk.

My heart jumps in shock at his reaction.

I bite back the terror. 'Well, I'm sorry, Papa. I mean no disrespect to you.

I love you, but you cannot force me against my will. I'm not a child anymore. I don't want to marry a man with such taste. It will disgust me to be with him.'

He stares at me and studies me as if I am a different species from him and he must decide what technique would work best on me. He stands and comes around the side of the desk. I resist the urge to flinch when he stops next to me. His body radiates a strong aura of something I find utterly repulsive.

'Do you know that I was the first one to call you by the nickname *solnyshko*?' he asks softly.

I shake my head, confused by his sudden change of demeanor.

He smiles. 'So no one told you the story. Well, I called you that because I was at your birth and I saw your head—you were born with a full head of gold hair—appear out of that bitch's cunt and, I swear, it looked like the sun coming out of the depths of night. So I called you little sun. My little sun. Until today you have been my perfect little sun. You can ruin it all in one stroke.'

'I just—'

His powerful hands reach out suddenly and grip my shoulders. I am unable to stifle the scream of shock and fright. In an instant he pulls me forward until my face is only inches from his. I smell the coffee he drank on the plane, the cigar he smoked on the way home.

'Think about the people you care for, little sun. They all depend on you to survive. This one selfless act could mean so much for their future ... existence.' He pauses and takes stock of the reaction I am unable to conceal. He reminds me of a snake, extending its tongue to sense the vulnerability of its prey.

I understand that he has left the most important words unsaid. 'Papa, I can't—'

'If you defy me, Tasha, you will leave me no choice. Those you love the most will suffer the consequences.'

I gasp at the unveiled threat. 'What are you saying?'

'Who do you love most in this world, *solnyshko*?'

The loving nickname on his lips suddenly sounds grotesque. Baba, Mama ... Surely, he couldn't be referring to them. I shake my head in disbelief.

'I'll rub them out one by one.'

His words are like a dagger to my heart. I choke back my growing sense of helplessness. I have to free myself from his clutches. He could be bluffing. He must be. 'I'm your daughter. How can you threaten me like this, Papa?'

'I do what is necessary to get what I want.'

'Only a monster could be so cruel,' I cry tearfully.

'What do you know, you silly girl? You're nothing more than a spoilt brat.'

'I'm not a spoilt brat.'

His eyes flash with annoyance. 'No? You agreed to this alliance. And now after you have turned everybody's life upside down you have changed your mind. You are an Evanoff and we keep our word. Nothing will stop this alliance. You should know I mean every word when I tell you no one you love is safe. No one. Unless you submit to my wish.'

I open my mouth and my father lifts his hand and waves me away as if I have already taken up too much of his time.

'By the way, don't imagine that I do not know about your visits to that bitch. Tell your grandmother if she throws the rope ladder for you again to go visit her, I'll send her back to Russia with only the clothes on her back.'

My jaw drops with shock. Would Papa really do that to his own mother? Impossible. Yet, I feel chilled to the bone. My mother was right. How could I have been so oblivious to the fact that the man who provides everything for me and protects me day and night is completely heartless.

There is no point in even trying to talk to him. He loves no one. He can't. He is unable to. He is like the spoon or the table.

Like that he feels nothing.

Twenty-seven

Tasha Evanoff

https://www.youtube.com/watch?v=nVjs
GKrE6E8
Summertime Sadness

'Did you ever say goodbye to someone
knowing it would be forever?'
-Tasha Evanoff

I dress in red. My mother says blondes should always dress in red when they want to be sexy. I stand in front of the mirror but I don't look sexy. I look pale and washed out. Blusher. More blusher. That's what I need. I pick up the blusher brush and dust color on the apple of my cheeks.

And what of your eyes? What can be done with sadness in them?

I turn away from the mirror.

I bend down and kiss Sergei. 'This is my last time so no guilt trips from you, you hear?' I tell him.

He whimpers and I pull him into my arms for a hug. He remains very still and when I pull away he cries.

'Be a good boy and wait for me, okay?'

I stand and he stands too. To my surprise he barks at me.

'Shhh … no barking. Everybody is sleeping,' I say, quickly getting back down on the floor and hugging him tightly once again. I understand why he is like this. He is picking up on my distress.

'It's okay,' I coax. 'I'm fine. I will be fine. This feeling will pass. Everything can be forgotten. I'll be back in the morning and we'll go walkies in the park. Be a good boy for mummy, okay?'

I give him a treat, but he refuses to eat it.

'I'll just leave it here, and you eat it later when you feel like it, hmmm?'

I kiss him again and walk to the door, but he follows and whimpers pitifully and cries as if I have physically hurt him when I close the door. I stand for a moment hearing him scratching at the wood and feeling terrible, then knowing that there is nothing I can do about it, I take my shoes off and go down the stairs.

The house is so quiet I can hear my heart hammering in my chest. I was never risking anything except my father's displeasure before. If discovered, what I am doing now is dangerous to all the people I love most. I always thought my father loved me in his own way, but now I know. I am just a pawn in his game. I have no value to him beyond opening a door to the most esteemed echelons of society.

Fortunately, the nervousness and that sinking feeling that everything is going to go wrong doesn't translate into anything bad. I scale the wall easily in my red dress, the taxi is waiting at the end of the road, and before I know it I am standing outside Noah's door. I ring it and he opens it.

Even though I am smiling at him, he takes one look at my face and asks, 'What's wrong?'

'Now that I'm here, nothing. Absolutely nothing,' I lie.

He pulls me in as his eyes roam my body. 'You look fabulous,' he murmurs, nuzzling my neck. There is music in the background. *When A Man Loves A Woman* is playing.

I don't want to cry. I don't want to be sad. I just want to hide in a dance and a smile. 'Will you dance with me?' I whisper. *A last dance. To forget my great misery.*

He lifts his head and smiles softly. 'Does the pope pray?'

I smile as he tightens his arms around me and we move slowly in time to the music. I bury my face in his neck and inhale the lovely male scent of him.

'Sergei didn't want me to come tonight,' I whisper.

He pulls a little away to look at me. 'Why not?'

I don't know for sure.

'Are you going to tell me what's wrong or am I going to have to use my secret method of extracting information,' he teases, even though his eyes are actually very serious.

'You're going to have to use the secret method,' I tell him.

'Right. You asked for it.'

He picks me up and carries me to the bedroom.

I laugh while my heart cries, *don't leave me.*

He puts me on the bed and looks down at me. His eyes are dark and hungry. 'God, you're so beautiful, Tasha,' he says, his exhaled breath almost a hiss.

'I don't want you to use a condom. I want to feel you come inside me. I want you to fill me with cum.'

He narrows his eyes. 'Are you protected?'

I shake my head.

'But—'

I grasp his hand urgently. 'It's what I want.'

'Are you sure?'

'I've never been more sure of anything in my life.'

Very gently he removes my dress and my underwear. Then he begins to kiss every nook and cranny of my body. Every inch, every tip, every swollen bit of flesh, every wet thing, until my body feels as soft as warm butter, and I feel as if I have no will of my own. I feel the heat seep into my pussy as if I've been sitting with my legs open for a long time in the sun.

'How do you feel?' he asks.

'Mmmm.' I can't speak. My sex-hazed mind can't even think. I let out a small moan as I feel the thick head of his cock enter me. My muscles wrap around it eagerly.

'How does this feel?' I ask, squeezing his shaft.

'Tight, hot, and wet.' He pushes all the way in.

'Fuck,' we both say in unison.

'I love watching my cock disappear into you,' he growls as he jams into me hard.

'Don't let me go, Noah.' The words in my heart slip out of my mouth.

He stops moving. We stare at each other. 'Understand something, Tasha. I will never give up on you or let you go, no matter how hard it gets. You are my woman. I will cover your body with my death if I have to.'

And just like that the tears begin to flow out of my eyes.

'Tasha, what's the matter?'

I shake my head. 'Don't stop.'

He looks down at me worriedly. 'Are you all right?'

He tries to pull out of me, but I grab his hips. 'No. Don't stop. Please finish. Please make me come. Make it the most beautiful sex we've ever had.'

'I can't. Not when you're crying ...'

'I'm fine. Honestly. Please. For me.' The tears run freely down my temples as I struggle to master my emotions.

He looks down at me, a strange expression on his face, then he plunges back into me, going as deeply as he can. I look at his face, contorted with passion and I memorize it. The day will come when these twilight hours when I have been so happy, will no longer fill me with grief. Then I will learn the art of being happy that I had them at all. For they are a gift. I will weather the winter and one day, April will come again.

Slowly, I become completely consumed with the intense feeling rushing through me that I notice even the littlest change in his face. I see he is ready to climax, but he can think only of making me come.

His thrusts become rougher and more forceful as he slides in and out of me. I see his breathing quicken, his nostrils flare, and the muscles of his neck and shoulders work as he pumps into me. His eyes stare into mine, wanting, needing me to come. He won't let go until I do.

I feel the climax approaching as if from a long tunnel, almost, but not quite there. I realize it's not going to come. Not when I'm in this mood.

'Sorry. I don't think I can come,' I apologize.

'There's no rush. Just relax and let it come, Tasha.'

All his muscles are tight. His control is barely leashed. 'Don't wait for me,' I whisper.

'You're coming with me, or nobody is coming tonight,' he says, his brow clinched together in concentration.

He bends his head and sucks my nipples causing a jolt of electrifying pleasure in my body. My brain becomes cloudy. My fingers clench into his shoulders. The jolts of sensation magnify in intensity. I groan and he increases the pace of his thrusts.

I wrap my legs around his hips and let go, come what may.

His movements become even harsher and faster.

The train starts hurtling towards me until it body slams into me and the strangest thing happens. For a moment I disappear. The moment is infinitesimally small, but its impact is massive. During that second I'm no longer me, an individual, or confined to my body. I dissolve into the unity of the all, knowing no limitation, infinite.

There it is, the true secret of sexual orgasm in its purest form.

Melting and becoming one with the trees, the stars, the sky, the rocks, the ocean, the man inside your body. It is merging. The sinner and the sage, the good into bad, night into day, death into life, and back again. That single moment without distinction is holier than spending years in a monastery or temple. It is that moment Baba spoke of when you enter a lake and meet your own soul.

Then the moment is over and I am just a woman underneath her man.

I look into his eyes and they are so ... so very sad. I want to reach out a hand and touch his cheek. I want to tell him I love him, but I can do neither, my hands are immobilized, and my mouth will not move.

I look up at him from underneath drenched lashes. He seems very still, resting on his elbows, his breathing deep and heavy as he stares down at me.

Twenty-eight

Tasha Evanoff

https://www.youtube.com/watch?v=bqIx
CtEveG8
Beneath Your Beautiful

'**H**ave I hurt you?' he asks softly.

I blink in amazement. 'No,' I whisper. 'Of course not.'

'Then tell me why you're crying.'

'I'm crying because everything has been just beautiful. I couldn't have asked for more.'

He trails his fingertips down my cheek. 'It will be all right. You'll see. I'll make it good for us.'

I want to burst into tears, but I don't. I nod.

'Will you trust me?'

I nod again.

'I'll sort it out. I promise.'

'Okay. I need to go to the bathroom,' I say.

He moves and I get up. I pick up my dress and underwear from the floor and go into the bathroom. I close the door and lean against it. I thought I was going to stay all night. I thought I could do it, but I can't. My heart is breaking. I can't stay here a moment longer. My legs give way and my body slides down to the floor.

'Tasha,' Noah calls from outside.

I press the heel of my hand against my teeth. 'Just give me a minute,' I say.

I hear him walk away.

I stand up and dress quickly. My hands shake so much I can hardly pull the zipper up. I run my finger through my hair then, squaring my shoulders, go out into the room. He is sitting on the bed, and he has pulled on his sweatpants.

'What's up?' he asks, his face expressionless.

I exhale the breath I'm holding. 'I should go home.'

'Yeah?'

I take a step towards him and shrug. 'And I won't be coming back again.'

His eyes narrow. 'Why not?' he asks calmly.

I swallow hard. 'This was meant to be a temporary arrangement, after all. My father is back and really it's time things went back to the way they were. It was only meant to be one night, but you're very good in bed and it was fun so ...' I trail away.

He stands up and starts walking towards me, and I don't think, I just run. I get as far as the door before he catches me and slams me up against the wall. Not hard enough to hurt, but just enough to shock.

'Why are you running?' he asks curiously. There is something eerily calm about him.

'Will you please let go of me?'

'After you've answered my question.'

'Let go of me first.'

'Just answer the question, Tasha,' he sighs.

'Look, it's finished. We've both had our fun and now I'm going back to Oliver. Don't make this difficult.'

'You're going back to Jarsdale?' He says each word slowly.

'He *is* my fiancé, and you knew that.'

He smiles nastily. I've never seen him smile at me like that ever. 'That's a funny thing to say while you got more of my DNA inside you than an episode of CSI.'

'Don't make me dislike you.'

His eyes widen. 'Dislike? How about I make you hate me?'

In a flash he has stuck his hand under my skirt and ripped my panties off my body.

I slap him hard. It just happens. My hand rises up, flies in the air, connecting with his cheek. And it isn't one of those girl slaps either. It cracks in the air, makes his head jerk, and leaves my handprint on his cheek.

His eyes glitter as he smiles slowly. 'Your father shouldn't have bothered with a paternity test. You're his daughter all right.'

My knees start trembling, and my mouth opens with shock. He is like a stranger. So cruel. He's never spoken to me like that. I have never seen this side of him. Just because he has always been so gentle, kind, and considerate I had the false illusion that there isn't another side to him. Or rather, I chose to ignore the side of him that has hurt, killed, and maimed. Perhaps I don't know him at all.

He and my father are from the same world, after all.

'Noah,' I cry, my voice hoarse with hurt and horror at the beast I have unleashed. My shaking hands reach out for him.

Suddenly his mouth is on mine, crushing, rough, possessive, demanding, taking. He forces his tongue into my mouth, hooks my tongue with it and, pulling it into his own, sucks it hard. I whimper as his leg parts my thighs, and his hand moves upwards to find my slick entrance. His fingers slide in, and he begins to pump them in and out of me. I'm so wet his fingers make a squelching sound. He lifts his head.

'Started to hate me yet?' he asks.

'I hate you.' The words tremble in the air between us.

'Who should I believe? Your body is telling me a different story,' he snarls.

He lifts me in his arms and carries me to his bed. The covers feel cold against my heated skin.

'What are you going to do?' I ask stupidly.

He laughs a little. 'Little innocent Tasha,' he taunts.

He pushes down his sweatpants and he is hard and erect. He gets on the bed.

'You are mine,' he growls harshly as he thrusts deep into me. I groan and he puts his fingers slick with my juices into my mouth, making me suck them. My fingers grasp the cool sheet under me as he quickens his speed. He stares at me, and unable to bear his gaze, I close my eyes.

'Open your eyes,' he orders sternly.

My eyes fly open.

'Tell me you want me to stop.'

'I ... I ... ah ...'

'Tell me you want me to fuck you.'

'I want you to ... ah ... fuck you .... me, fuck me.'

'Tell me your pussy belongs to me.'

'My pussy belongs to you,' I cry.

'I didn't hear that.'

'My pussy belongs to you,' I scream uncontrollably as the waves of an incredible orgasm engulfs me. It rips through my very core like a hurricane. It drains me completely before it is over. I stare up at my gorgeous man as his body contracts and arches, and he goes off to meet his own climax.

He pulls out and cum gushes out of me.

'I have to go,' I whisper.

'I know. Let me call Sam.'

He gets off the bed and walks out of the room.

I go into the bathroom, clean myself, and go downstairs. He is standing by the drinks cabinet. There is a glass in his hand. I have a sense of déjà vu. I go into the room and stand in the middle of it.

'I'm sorry I said all those horrible things,' I admit.

He looks at me sadly. 'Don't apologize, Tasha. It was nothing. Between us there is nothing to be sorry for.'

'But I said such nasty things and made you so angry.'

'Do you really believe that just some silly words could change anything for me? I would die for you, Tasha Evanoff.'

I run sobbing into his arms. He holds me tight. 'My poor, poor Tasha,' he croons. He pulls me away from him slightly and strokes my hair. 'Don't come to see me anymore, OK? Leave it all to me. Don't do a single thing.'

I feel the pain of his words like a knife in my chest, but I nod.

 206

He kisses my wet eyelids one by one. 'I promise you'll be mine, or I'll die fucking trying.'

Like a fool I start sobbing again. I hardly ever cried before I met him. Now I'm like some sort of broken tap that can't stop gushing.

'Shhh ... my darling.'

'I don't want you to die,' I bawl.

'We all have to die. It's how we die that counts. I'm not afraid to die for you.'

'My father—'

'I'm not afraid of your father. I may have a card up my sleeve.'

I stop crying and stare at him. 'Really? What?'

He smiles. 'You seriously think I'm gonna tell you?'

'Give me a clue what it's about?'

'No.'

Then the taxi comes and he walks me to the street. At the open door of the cab our fingers linger. In the light of the streetlamps his face looks distant and sad. Both of us know this could be the last time. I kiss him on his cheek.

His skin is warm and bristly. I inhale the smell of him one last time and turn away blindly. The waterworks have started again.

Twenty-nine

Tasha Evanoff

https://www.youtube.com/watch?v=Ak7kedzR8bg
Ten Green Bottles

I leave my grandma in the kitchen enjoying her pot of tea, slip my shoes off, and I take the stairs two at a time. The house is still and gloomy. My father must still be asleep.

I open my door. I don't know why, but I have the craziest ... I mean it's just so stupid that I could even think something like that ... but I actually think Sergei is wrapped up in his blankets, so fast asleep he did not hear me come in.

The fantasy that he is asleep continues as I walk towards him. Even though the air in the room smells funny. Metallic and sweet. Even as I stand over him, my mind stubbornly refuses to believe what I am seeing.

Then it hits me and my legs give way beneath me. It feels as if I am under water. There are no sounds, there is resistance to my movements, and everything is happening in slow motion as I fall to my knees in front of him.

In slow motion my hand reaches out, grasps the edge of the blanket, lifts it, and that is the moment the slow dream ends. With a startled shriek of horror, I fall backwards onto my butt. In a mad panic fueled by terror and disbelief, I scramble away on the palms of my hands, my heels kicking, scrabbling, and scurrying on the ground like some demented four-legged animal. My back hits the wall and I stop. I sit propped up against it, breathing hard, and staring in utter shock at my beautiful, beautiful beheaded baby.

Someone came into my bedroom and *beheaded* my baby!

Chopped off his head.

It is completely severed from his body and whoever that sick monster was, he has placed Sergei's head at the end of his tail. It is the most grotesque sight I've ever seen in my life. Slowly, I crawl back to him.

'I'm sorry,' I whisper. 'I'm so sorry. I didn't mean to run away from you. I love you.'

I reach into his basket and my hand touches his fur. There is no more give to his still skin, so his fur feels hard and cold. I flinch. Sergei has been dead for a long time.

How he must have suffered.

How frightened he must have been.

There is an A4 size paper on his body wrapped around something. I unfurl it. It's one of those tiny tape recorders that bosses use to dictate things for their secretaries.

I read the note. Only three little words but they turn my heart into a fist of ice.

One by one.

In a daze I press play on the tape and the nursery song *Ten Green Bottles* starts playing. The innocent but strangely eerie children's song seems obscene beyond all words. The greatest insult to Sergei's

bloodied, mutilated body. I fling the tape to the wall and it crashes and opens. The tape flying out and bouncing. It falls close to the treat I gave Sergei.

He never ate it.

My hands clench with a sick helplessness.

I go to the bed, my knees knocking together, and pull the sheet off. I fold it into four and spread it in front of Sergei's little body. Kneeling in front of his bed, I bend down and pick him up. His severed head first. The congealed blood is like runny jelly underneath him. My hands immediately become dark red.

Tenderly, I lay his head on the sheet. Then I pick up his body. In death he is much heavier and I have to grunt to lift him. Once he is in my arms it is easier and I lay it next to his poor head so that both halves of him are joined.

Then I lay down beside him. 'I'm sorry. I'm sorry. I'm sorry,' I whisper again and again as I hug his cold, hard body. The guilt is terrible. I wasn't here to protect him. I was out having a good time. I should have been here. If I had only left him in Baba's room. I even thought about it and then I thought no, he might bark when I call or make a noise and wake Papa.

So I didn't leave him in her room.

He must have had a premonition. No wonder he whimpered and cried when I left. And I still left. I close my eyes and grit my teeth with regret.

I kiss the top of his head. I kiss his closed eyelids, and I hold his elegant bloodied, little paws. The pads used to feel soft and warm. They feel hard, rough, and cold. When his nose touches my lips it is dry and not wet with life.

I sit up and look down on him. It doesn't feel real. It can't be real. My mind is blank. I can't think. It is my fault. Poor Sergei. I cover his remains with the sheet and go to open a window.

Fresh morning air rushes in.

I think of Sergei running free in the park. I think of Sergei licking my face. I think of Sergei as a puppy hiding under the bed when he heard thunder and how I had picked him up, holding him in my arms, taking him to the window to show him that it was just a storm. There are no tears. I am too shocked to feel anything. Not even anger at my father.

I think of my father. How could he? He brought Sergei home for me. Having said Sergei always hated him.

I sit in my room hunched, confused, and immobilized with shock and horror, until I hear Baba come up the stairs. Then I run to the top of the stairs and she stops mid-step.

'What is it?' she asks, her hands roaming my bloodied clothes and hands.

'Sergei is dead,' I say.

Her reaction is instant and shocking. She goes white and her knees buckle so that she has to tighten her hold on the banister to stop herself from falling. She closes her eyes in pain. I run down the steps to where she is and take her hand.

'It's okay, Baba. It's okay,' I tell her, even though I want to lay my head on her chest and bawl my eyes out.

She catches my hand. 'How?'

I shake my head.

'Show me his body,' she demands suddenly.

I shake my head vigorously. 'No, don't look at him, Baba.'

'Is he in your room?'

I nod, because I am suddenly so choked up I cannot speak. It's the strangest thing, but while I am standing there with Baba, part of me doesn't believe that Sergei is actually dead. It's more possible that this is all a nightmare or a mistake. My brain can't comprehend that it could be real. He can't be gone. Just like that. It almost feels as if all I have to do is let my grandmother into my room, and she will not find my beloved dog cut into two pieces and wrapped up in a sheet.

Baba starts up the stairs, her face determined, and I follow.

I stand back as she opens the door, and for a few seconds just stands at the doorway. Then she walks towards the covered cloth and I go into the room and close the door. The air is freezing cold because I opened the window. My eyes fall on the sheet stained dark red.

That isn't my Sergei under there. He's gone.

I watch Baba get onto her haunches with difficulty, and lift the sheet. Silently I watch her sigh deeply and let the sheet drop back down. Then she looks up at me. Her eyes are totally blank and her face is like stone. I have never seen my grandmother look like this before.

'My son is a monster.'

I don't say anything. My eyes sting and my throat feels as if there is a stone in it.

'Whatever you want from me, just ask,' she says.

I swallow the stone. It goes down hard. 'Come for the funeral.'

Thirty

Tasha Evanoff

https://www.youtube.com/watch?v=RgK
AFK5djSk
See You Again

I'm afraid I fell apart after inviting my grandmother to Sergei's funeral. I ended up in bed crying like a baby. She arranged everything. She got a white pet casket delivered inside of an hour. It has a cross etched on the lid and it is satin lined. She put his favorite toys and blanket into it. She ordered flowers. White roses. She invited the staff to come.

We meet under the apple tree. The sky above is charcoal and a great storm is expected later. The gardener, John, has dug a hole. Nobody can meet my eyes. There is an air of shock and disbelief. The little Polish maid who helps the chef looks frightened. Her eyes dart about nervously.

Baba and I are dressed entirely in black. I hold a handkerchief to my trembling mouth while Baba says a little prayer. I watch everybody throw coins on top of the coffin.

I kneel down and throw the first clump of soil on his casket.

'My darling Sergei, please forgive me. Forgive me. Forgive me that I wasn't there to protect you,' I whisper softly. 'I know I promised that I wouldn't cry and make your spirit anxious, but I just can't bear this sorrow. Never mind, I'll see you again,' I say, and begin to stand, but I stumble backwards. I feel an arm come around my back.

'Don't shed further tears, Tasha. Love is eternal. He will love you from wherever he is,' Baba consoles, but her voice rings hollow in my ears.

Then everybody else throws their handful of dirt, and Baba comes to me. With her hand firmly around my waist she leads me away.

I let her take me back to the house. At the door she stops and holds out a hand. She is asking for my handkerchief.

It is our custom to throw away our used handkerchiefs after a funeral. It is a way of reminding the mourners that one's sorrows should start to diminish once the funeral has passed and not carried much farther into the future.

Automatically, I put my handkerchief into her hand.

'Shall we have some tea?' Baba asks, putting both our handkerchiefs in a plastic bag.

I shake my head. 'I'll just lie down for a while,' I say.

She smiles. 'Yes. Perhaps you should have a nap. I'll wake you up in a couple of hours and we can have lunch together.'

I nod vaguely and enter the house. The house is even more silent than it usually is. I feel a strange chill go through me at the deathly silence. I go upstairs to my room.

While I was out someone has cleaned the room. Sergei's bed is gone and the room smells of air freshener. I go to the window and watch John fill Sergei's grave. Shovel by shovel until the ground is level. I watch him stop, push his palms into the small of his back, then sit under the tree and light a cigarette. His life seems wonderfully simple and uncomplicated.

Never again to see those eyes.

Tears cloud my eyes as I turn away from the window and walk to the bed. I sit on it and feel as if I am hollow, all my insides eaten away. Sergei's little funeral has crushed my heart and broken my spirit in a way nothing before has done. I loved Sergei like he was part of me. He was always by my side other than the rare times I could not take him. I don't even feel real anymore.

I feel as if I am living in a dream.

How can it be anything but a dream, if one moment someone is warm and alive and real and the next they are just gone? Forever. You cannot see, touch, or hear them ever again. How can all of us walk about pretending life is real, that it couldn't at the drop of a hat pop into nothing?

What almighty arrogance to think that *I* of all people had anything in my control. What a joke. How my father must be laughing now. I believed, I actually believed, I could have my cake and eat it. I thought I could have Mama, Baba, Sergei, even Papa, and Noah. One big happy family. Fool. In one brutal stroke my father showed me different. I underestimated him.

Badly.

My father doesn't understand love, but he has a gift of manipulating the love others feel. He sees inside a heart, feels its greatest vulnerability, and attacks. Yes, he took my beloved Sergei from me, but I know Sergei died with his love for me intact forever and mine for him.

There is a soft knock on my door.

I walk to it and open it. Rosita is standing outside. 'Your father wants you to join him for lunch downstairs,' she says.

'Thank you, Rosita. Tell him I'll be down in a minute,' I say and close the door. He is home. I did not realize.

I lean against the door, feeling so numb that I cannot even begin to figure out why my father wants me to join him for lunch. Does he want to gloat? Does he want to frighten me more? Does he just want to have lunch with me because what he did to Sergei is not a big deal?

I straighten, open the door, and go downstairs towards the dining room. On the way I meet one of his men. He nods to me and I nod back automatically.

I open the dining room door and my father looks up and smiles. To look at him you would never believe that he sent someone up to his own daughter's bedroom to murder her dog so she would come home totally unsuspecting and find the slaughter. I don't smile back. I just stare at him. Shocked that all these years I never really knew him at all.

He puts his fork and knife down. 'Come in, come in,' he invites genially, still chewing his food.

I don't move.

He smiles. 'Just because it is delivered in a friendly tone do not regard my invitation as anything but a direct order.'

I walk stiffly into the room. My right palm is itching. I hold it in my left hand and scratch it furiously.

'Come closer,' he purrs. 'What are you afraid of?'

I take a few more steps.

He stands up and, bending down, takes something out of a cardboard box. To my absolute horror and disgust it is a blue Doberman puppy. My eyes bulge with shock. Surely not. The puppy is the exact age Sergei was when he gave him to me.

My eyes move slowly up to his.

'This is a present for you,' he says, jerking it slightly in my direction.

I stare at him dumbfounded. I thought my father was a monster, but he is not. To be a monster means you have feelings. My mother was right. My father has no feelings. He killed my beloved dog and now he is replacing it with a puppy. He can give then take it away and give it again. What a sick freak. Only a man who cannot feel love would do what he is doing. He jerks the puppy again to encourage me to take it.

I take a step back. 'I don't want it,' I say.

He scowls. 'If you don't take it I'll have to get the staff to drown it.'

My mouth drops open and he takes a step towards me with the puppy wriggling in his outstretched hands. I put my hands out and take it from him. Its body is soft and warm and I feel the tears start to burn the backs of my eyes.

I turn around so he will not see them and run out of the room. I stand for a

moment in the grand foyer. Rosita is on her hands and knees polishing the marble steps. I walk up to her.

The puppy makes a small sound that is not quite a bark yet. It tears at my heart. Sergei used to make that sound. It's not its fault. It's just an innocent little thing, but I can't even look at it. My heart is broken. I hold it out to her.

'Please can you take him and see that he is well taken care of.'

She looks at me with a surprised, confused face, but she puts her hands out and takes the puppy from me. I wipe my hands on the sides of my dress.

'Thank you, Rosita,' I croak, and run upstairs.

In my room I fall on my bed and sob my heart out. I don't even hear the door open, I only feel it when Baba's hand falls on my head and strokes my hair gently.

'I hate him,' I sob. 'I hate him so much.'

Baba says nothing, just hums an old Russian song she used to sing to put me to sleep when I was a child.

Thirty-one

Noah Abramovich

https://www.youtube.com/watch?v=N6v oHeEa3ig
Gangster Paradise

They were waiting for me in the shadows. The punch catches me in an area just above the ear, and in the confusion, my brain registers it merely as a thud, but in fact, it's the kind of blow you never want to get hit with.

It's fucking lethal. You can't prepare, or train for it.

It's where the expression 'knocked senseless' originates from. I've been clipped like this once during training while I was preparing myself with the worst case scenarios, so I know how this shit goes down.

Seconds later, it scrambles my senses. My eyes blur, the world starts spinning, and I lose control of my legs as they turn to jelly. I'm going down and all that matters now is how hard. Fall on my head and everything could go dark and silent. Maybe even forever.

'Fuck,' I yell, as I try to position my hands out in front of me to cushion the fall.

I'd always imagined my end would be bloody. You live by the sword you die by the damn thing. It's the unwritten rule and it's fair. It should be that way. Even time spent in prison doesn't change anything, they are only pauses, before this gory and fitting finale. A bullet in the head, a knife in the gut in a dark alleyway.

Yeah, I see it now, not parking in the gym's car park was a really bad idea. Careless. Careless. Zane was right. While you're finding the gentleman's way of taking care of the solution, he'll just fucking send someone around to snuff you out.

Then a sane voice in my head. *Get a grip Noah, if they wanted you dead, you'd already be! You're still breathing.*

'Fucking put that piece away. What are you, fucking stupid? Get your fucking knife out you pussy, and slice him up good. Boss said, make mincemeat out of his face. And hurry the fuck up about it.'

I hear a man's voice spit with disgust.

So that's their fucking game. A message from the father of the bride: mess with my daughter and I'll leave you clinging to life and marked forever, unable to walk amongst normal people. You can't argue with the strategy. It has the added benefit of being a good way to cool down a girl's ardor too.

I hear the sound of a knife blade swish open. It is like an electric shock to my brain. It makes me focus and gets my head together. They're all fucking tooled up, but I'll kill these fuckers before I accept anyone telling me who I can and can't have as my woman.

Before I breathe my last I'll be sure to pay a less than friendly visit to that filthy pervert her father has chosen for her. Just thinking of it is enough to get the adrenaline to break through the fog in my brain, and race around my body again. There's three of them.

I can take them.

As my eyes begin to clear and I spy two trouser legs approaching, a thick hand grasping a sliver of cold steel. I don't let my gaze go further up.

Get up Noah, get the fuck up now.

'Ready for a bit of free plastic surgery, loverboy?' he taunts.

I gather up every bit of power inside me and thrust all my weight behind a powerful kick aimed straight at his shin bone, at that weak point just under the knee. Shame I'm not wearing my heavy boots, but even so I hear the crack of bone as it tears through flesh. It's beautiful music to me. He falls to the ground screaming like a girl.

One down.

I spring to my feet, just as I am confronted by two large soldiers rushing towards me. One is built like a brick shithouse, the other tall, lean, and mean. A scar running right across his neck. Their features make me think they're probably from Chechnya. Tough, ruthless men.

Fuck them.

Fuck you, Nikita.

Every nerve ending in my body feels alive and on fire as I dodge the tall guy's knife by ducking below his blow. As it whizzes by, I land a hard body punch to his solar plexus. It sends him flying to the ground, crippled, breathless, and in agony.

The ruthless killer in me takes over.

I yank his blade from his hand, step behind his arched body, and with neither thought nor mercy, pull his head back and finish the job some other man had started. I put the tip of the blade to the bottom of his ear and open him ear to ear. Hot blood flows down my hands. He makes wet gurgling sounds, gasps uselessly for air, then slumps.

Two down. I let him drop out of my hands. He lands with a thud.

One more to go, but he's the boss. He's the one I have to watch out for.

Before I can turn around he attacks, and lands a hard blow to my ribs. It winds me temporarily, and leaves me gasping for air. Another man would have gone down, but not me. I summon every last bit of strength I have and straighten as he comes at me again. He is like a mountain, but I have agility on my side. I sidestep his lunge and catch him full in the face with my elbow, smashing his nose to a bloody pulp.

His hands instinctively shoot up to cover his face, but before he has time to gather his senses, I grab his right wrist with both hands and smash my knee into his groin. With a near-soundless grunt of white hot pain, he stumbles and collapses to the ground cupping his junk. In a flash, I fall on his body and straddle him.

He realizes his mistake and starts struggling, his arms flailing, trying to hit at anything. He is no match for my force of momentum, as I plunge the knife he dropped deep into his chest. His eyes widen and he makes a muffled, slow choking sound. Blood bubbles in his mouth and runs out of the side. I sit on him, panting hard, and watch the light die out of his eyes. I thought I'd never have to see the life go out of another man at my hands, but Tasha is worth it. I'd kill hundreds more like him for her.

I turn my head slowly and glance at the man with the broken tibia. He is still lying on the ground, white bone jutting through flesh, and staring at me with bulging eyes. Quickly, I rifle the pockets of the dead man underneath me, locate and retrieve his mobile phone. I scroll down to the last number and, sucking air in my lungs, walk over to where the first man is lying, looking at me with a mixture of hate and fear.

I thrust the mobile into his face. 'Call your boss.'

He looks at me without blinking.

'Call him or join your friends in hell.'

He looks around at his dead mates' blood-soaked bodies, weighs up the situation, and grimaces. 'You might as well kill me. I'm as good as dead if I call him anyway.' I underestimated him. He's a good judge of character. He'd rather take his chances with me than Nikita.

I press the button and hold the phone to my ear.

'What?' Tasha's father barks.

'Nikita, you're losing your touch.'

There is a pause, then he speaks. His voice is deliberately pleasant and unruffled even though I know he must be fucking furious. 'Well, well, I wasn't expecting to hear your voice, Noah.'

'You must be getting old, Nikita, sending boys to a do a man's work.'

'Listen you little upstart low life. Come near my daughter again and I'll fucking kill you myself.'

The idea of Nikita killing me makes me laugh. As if he's ever done his own wet work.

'Let see how you laugh when your mouth is full of concrete.'

'Well, if I were you I'd stop with the weird fantasies, and deal with the more pressing scenario you've got going on here. It might be a good idea to get your garbage disposal people over, like pronto, before the cops are all over it.'

I hear his brain turning over.

'You should pray that I don't turn up dead, even by accident. Because the cops will be getting a USB stick detailing the exact money trail of that drug deal gone wrong. Remember Hammurabi?'

He doesn't say anything but I can feel his shock. Zane and I got a copy ages ago, and we just kept it for insurance purposes. You never know when you need these things.

'I'll be seeing you real soon, Nikita.' I say, and hang up.

I turn my attention back to the man on the ground.

'Please, please don't kill me,' he begs. 'It's not personal. We had orders. I'm sorry.'

Yeah, sure he's sorry. He's playing me for a chump. He's sorry I'm standing over him, he's sorry his friends can't help him, and he's sorry his busted leg means he can't run away.

I feel my adrenaline stop pumping as I stand above him, knife in hand. He eyes me fearfully and curls up like a child, sniveling, begging for mercy. Acting!

'You're a soldier you knew the risks,' I tell him.

I squeeze the handle. I can't kill a wounded, helpless man in cold blood. Anyway, he is more valuable alive than dead.

'I'll let you live so you can pass a message on to your boss.'

He nods violently.

'Tell him Tasha Evanoff belongs to me, and I will kill every man that is sent to come between us.'

I reach down with one hand and grab him by his trembling neck. With my other hand I draw my blade slowly and purposefully along his cheek, from ear to mouth. As the blade tears his flesh he howls out an awful scream. It ricochets through the emptiness of the alleyway.

When I am done I let him sink to the ground by my feet.

'Remember,' I snarl. 'If I ever see you again. I will kill you.'

I step away from him, remove a handkerchief from my jacket, and wipe the handle and blade clean of my fingerprints. That's when I see the bright crimson stain that is spreading over my ribs and down to my abdomen.

I wasn't fast enough. I've been stabbed, and it looks pretty fucking bad. I chuck the knife to the ground and try to walk, but my legs feel like they don't belong to me. I feel breathless after just a few steps. The adrenaline and fear kept me from feeling the pain before, but now it hurts like hell. Wincing, I lurch forward.

I just need to reach my car.

I'll call Zane. I push my hand into my jacket pocket to pull out my phone, and shit, fuck, my hand won't obey the commands of my brain. I don't want to be here when Nikita's men turn up. Life won't be worth living. Now what the fuck do I do? Taking in a deep breath that feels like I've swallowed fire, I grab onto the wall and try to pull myself along, but the life is quickly draining from my body.

Twenty more steps, Noah.

You can do it.

Come on.

I think of Tasha and her warm sweet smile. I want to live. I need to live. Fuck, I'm not going to make ...

Come on, Noah.

In my mind the sky is blue, the sun is shining, the ocean under Tasha and me is turquoise. 'Look, Noah. We're flying,' she cries.

Unable to stand upright any longer, I fold to the ground. I stare at the night sky. The stars in the sky look so beautiful. Everything is still. Baboshka's face is looking down at me. She is calling me. Then I hear footsteps. Getting closer, louder.

A face floats above me. Blue eyes. The bluest eyes I've ever seen. It is one of the saints or angels Baboshka prays to. He has come to take me to her.

Oh, Tasha. I don't want to leave, not yet, I had so many dreams for us, but I can't stay. They've come for me. I love you ....

Thirty-two

Tasha Evanoff

https://www.youtube.com/watch?v=xwt
dhWltSIg
Losing My Religion

The next day I call Noah's phone numerous times, but it is switched off all day and all night. I try not to worry. His battery died. He lost his phone. But my heart knows it is not that. He would never switch his phone off. Not at a time like this.

I call his club, The Matrix, put on an American accent, and pretend that I am Dahlia, Alexander Malenkov's wife. I ask to speak to Noah and the manager tells me nobody has heard from him since last night. He hasn't called any of his other businesses which is very weird.

'I'll get him to call you as soon as he calls in,' he says.

'No. No need,' I say quickly. 'I'll call him tomorrow.'

I sit on my bed and think. I think of all the possibilities that are open to me. Then I lay my plans meticulously. I play with a best case scenario and a worst case. I make a list of every move I plan to make, then I make a list of everything that can go wrong on every single move. Then I think up things that can go wrong outside of my actions.

At eight I go down to dinner and act normal. After dinner I go up to Baba's room and I tell her what I want to do. Step by step. She doesn't say a word. When I finish talking she puts her hand gently on my head. I know it is her way of giving me her blessing. I take her hand in my own and bringing it to my lips, kiss it.

Later when the household goes to sleep, Baba comes to my room, and I slip out of the house and climb the wall. I tell the cab driver to take me to Noah's house. As we drive up to the road I see it in complete darkness. I don't react. It is something I have already planned for. My whole body feels cold. I don't think about what has happened to him. If I do, I will just want to give up and die too.

The car comes to a stop. The driver turns to look at me.

My stomach is in knots. 'I've changed my mind. Take me to Rusaki. Rusaki is Dimitri Semenov's club. It is a Russian stripper club located in the underbelly of the city.

This is it now, Tasha. There's no going back.

I know I have to see it through to the very end. I turn my attention to the night traffic whizzing by until the cab driver pulls up outside its gaudy red and gold awning.

'We're here my love,' the taxi driver says.

I feel my heartbeat rise a notch as I take a deep breath and step out of the car. I pass the driver his money and thank him. Gathering my coat tightly around myself in an unconsciously defensive gesture I turn around to face the club's neon lights. As I walk up to it, I realize what I am doing I let go. Tilting my chin and letting my hands swing confidently, I go up to the entrance. There are three bouncers in black suits watching me approach with various expressions, leering, admiring, and expressionless.

I'm met by the large outstretched palm of the expressionless one. 'Dancers to the side door,' he says in a strong Russian accent, jerking his head towards a grey side door.

Beside me an obviously wealthy Russian man in a camel hair coat and an icy blonde on each arm is respectfully ushered in.

'I'm not a dancer.'

The leering one comes forward. 'What are you then?' he asks. His accent is English.

'I'm here to see Dimitri Semenov.'

The leering guy sniggers. 'Sorry darlin'. Even if you suck my cock you can't hope to see him.'

I stare at him as haughtily as I can, as my father would have done.

Keeping my expression blank I issue my instruction. 'Tell him Tasha Evanoff is here to see him.'

'I don't care if you're the Queen of England, you're not going in, little pussycat.'

'Did you say Evanoff,' the expressionless bouncer cuts in suddenly.

'Yes.'

The bouncer who was laughing at his own joke stops suddenly.

'You're Nikita Evanoff's daughter,' he repeats incredulously.

'That's right.'

'Got any ID to prove that?'

I hand over my driver's license.

He looks at it. 'I'll just hold on to this for a minute.'

'Of course,' I say coolly.

He unhooks the red rope and stands aside. 'I'm sorry about my colleague's behavior, Miss Evanoff,' he says in Russian. 'He didn't know who you were and meant no harm. He's English.'

'Of course,' I say graciously.

'Perhaps you'd like a drink while I tell him you are here.'

'Thank you, no,' I say.

As I follow him I hear the rude bouncer ask the admiring bouncer, 'Who the hell is Nikita Evanoff?'

I don't hear his reply.

'Please wait here,' he says, and disappears into a dark door.

I look around me. I've never been to a strip club. There is something sad and desperate about the women and the men. Both moving towards each other like magnets but connected only by the currency of money. I watch a woman on a pole.

'Come this way please,' the bouncer says close to my ear.

I follow him and we walk in silence along a darkened hallway, the sounds of our footsteps on the wooden floors creating an eerie feel. I feel my stomach churn again. At the end of the hallway we take a lift to the top. The door opens to a large room that wouldn't have looked out of place in a French palace. It is a startling contrast to the rest of the club.

'I'm going to have to frisk you, I'm afraid,' he says politely.

I hold my arms out as he brushes his hands down my sides, under my breasts, around my waist, and down my thighs. He stops at my knees. He is very professional about it, and I feel as cold as ice.

'This way,' he says. He opens a set of double doors and we enter a large expensively decorated room.

Dimitri Semenov is sitting on a long sofa with two topless blonde girls wearing thongs. They look frightened. I imagine them to be girls trafficked from Ukraine or Russia. He is carelessly fondling the breasts of one of them, as he watches me with small, curious eyes.

'Come in and sit down, Tasha,' he invites cordially.

Then in a completely psychotic about-turn he harshly orders the man who had shown me in to get out.

My eyebrows rise in surprise and he smiles. A sly, ugly smile. A shudder goes through me. I have heard this man is an utterly ruthless monster. I also know that other than me, no one hates my father more than him, and I have come to see him because of the old maxim.

The enemy of my enemy is my friend.

'So what can I do for Nikita's beloved only daughter?' He says the words as if he slurping them. He can hardly hide his delight that I have come to see him. He understands exactly what it means when your enemy's daughter comes to see you.

'I cannot speak to you in the presence of anyone else,' I say quietly.

He slaps the breast he was just fondling. 'You heard her. What are you waiting for?' Both women jump up and literally run out of the room.

He picks up his glass of amber liquid and takes a sip. 'There you go. Just you and me. Now speak.'

'I need to hire two of your most silent men for a day.'

His eyes narrow. 'All my men are silent.' Then to make sure that he has not misunderstood the situation he asks, 'Does your father know you are here?'

I shake my head

He smiles slowly. 'What sort of ... expertise should they possess?'

'Heavy lifting. They must be able to lift, help transport, and completely dispose of a heavy object.'

His smile widens even further. 'Do you know I have a pig farm? Those greedy beasts will eat anything. Back in Russia we used to feed them sawdust. Naturally, they enjoy a change to their diet as much as the next man.' His eyes glitter with cruelty.

'How much will it cost me?' I ask

'For Nikita Evanoff's daughter ... nothing,' he declares grandly, then he laughs again with the glee of knowing he is looking at the face of the instrument of his enemy's downfall.

Thirty-three

Tasha Evanoff

https://www.youtube.com/watch?v=W_r
Z9rHFwGY
You Ruin Me

It is not I, but Baba who invites my father to join us for dinner. He might have thought it suspicious if the invitation came from me, but since it is Baba, Baba who has loved him ever since he was born, Baba, who would have walked over hot coals for him, it never crosses his mind that she is inviting him to his last supper. He simply assumes she is trying to make peace between her warring kin.

To seal the deal, she tells him that the Chef is preparing his favorite pork *shashlik*, chunks of barbequed meat marinated in pomegranate juice.

He comes in smiling, confident ... happy. Not a thought for the harmless, innocent dog he butchered. Not just any creature. My baby. It's not even like he didn't know how much I adored that dog. I look up at him in wonder. This is my father. Incredible how he had completely brainwashed and manipulated me into accepting what he did to my mother.

It is almost as if the love he deliberately withheld from me put me under a spell where all I wanted to do was obey him and please him. Or perhaps my sub-conscious mind assimilated that scene with my mother better than I properly understood it. Fall out of line and get kicked out of the house forever. So I became the bird in a gilded cage. The world assumed I sang, but I was gray inside.

If I hadn't had the courage to turn up at Noah's office that night I might still be under his spell. But I've had a taste of what lies outside the cage. He crossed the line when he murdered my Sergei. I will never forgive him for that.

He looks at me directly and smiles. 'You look well, *solnyshko*.'

'Thank you, Papa,' I reply with lowered eyes.

He asks our server to bring him two bottles of Tsimlansky Black. Baba approves. The smoky, dusty red redolent with the smell of forest floor is perfect with chargrilled meat.

The wine is uncorked and left to breathe, and our glasses are filled with anisette. My father raises his glass and makes a toast.

'To the wealth of this family.'

I dutifully throw the drink down my throat.

He looks directly at me. 'One day, you will understand me.'

We stare at each other and suddenly we are locked in a vortex. There is no one else but us in this spinning world. The powerful bonds of love, hate, fear, loyalty, duty, deceit keeps us joined together as we swirl inexorably. Surely it must be clear to him that I am the child who has turned against its own father? It is impossible that he has not guessed his meek daughter and loving mother are about to kiss his cheek and betray him. I can't breathe. My lungs feel as if they are bursting.

Then he turns his eyes away from mine and reaches for a piece of black bread. I exhale the breath I was holding slowly. I look at his flushed face and, no, he has no idea. We are only chess pieces on his board. His arrogance would never allow him to believe that we could pick up our own skirts and move ourselves, or the other pieces.

The wine is poured, the food is brought in. There is not just *shashlik* but *kulebyakas* (pies made with meat, chicken, and cheese), a variety of blinis, pastries, fritters, meat jellies, pate, boneless duck with cucumber, two types of *ukhas* (soup). It is clear that each dish has been lovingly prepared and beautifully presented.

How I do, I do not know, but I consume the feast. As does Baba. Once my father stops to take a phone call, my eyes collide with Baba's and my heart stops. For an instant, it looks as if she has changed her mind, and cannot bring herself to go through with our plan, but then she forces herself to smile at me. It is a relief to know that seeing Papa at his most charming has not changed her mind.

The desserts arrive, chocolate mousse another favorite of Papa's. A sweet Hungarian wine Tokaj is opened and our glasses filled.

More anisette is poured, more toasts are made.

Baba looks at papa. 'Where there is love, there is no sin,' she says. We down our drinks.

He fills our glasses again. 'To love,' Papa says, holding his glass out to Baba.

'To long life,' I say, and we empty our glasses again. The alcohol burns my throat.

Then I watch him eat the mousse. He appears to enjoy it and not notice the aftertaste of the pills I got from Dimitri. I had been worried he would detect it, but he has eaten and drunk so much his senses have been significantly dulled. By the time coffee is served my father starts slurring his words. Baba asks one of the servants to help him up to his room.

Most of the servants start preparing to go home.

I go to my room and change into jeans, a T-shirt, and a thick sweater and sneakers.

10.15pm: it is the change-over time. For now only a skeleton staff of two guards at the entrance and, of course, the prowling dogs. Then in less than an hour all stations, back, front and sides, will be fully manned again.

10.20pm: I go out and call to the dogs. I bring them into the storeroom where I have put meat left over from our meal and close them in. Then I jam the camera by putting a piece of wood on the arm that moves it on its one-hundred-and-eighty-degree journey. It is unlikely that the men in the guardhouse will notice that the camera has stopped turning. If they do, I'm dead.

I wait.

10.30: I throw the rope ladder over the wall. Dimitri's men, Kiri and Vasluv, all dressed in black, climb silently over the wall. I pull the rope ladder back. I point at the stick holding the camera from moving and one of the men pulls it off. We slip into the dark kitchen and put the rope ladder and the stick into the bag.

10.34: I lead them to my father's room and stand watching as they inject my father with a longer lasting, deeper sedative. Then they pick him up and carry him down the stairs. They stop at the front door and wait for me.

10.40: I go out to the storeroom and let the dogs loose.

10.45. I see first the dogs, then both guards, their alarms bleeping, their guns at the ready, racing towards the back entrance. The computer screen is showing the back entrance has been breached. There may be an intruder in the grounds.

10.46: Baba cuts the electricity. The entire house goes dark. The cameras stop working. With my heart pounding I run out to my father's car start the engine, and open the trunk. The two men carry my father out of the house. They move surprisingly quickly considering my father's bulk. They stuff my father into the trunk and close it. Vasluv uses the key to open the electric gates that are stuck shut without electricity. Then he waits for us by the gates. Oh, shit. I see that one of my father's socks has dropped to the ground.

'The sock,' I whisper, pointing to it lying on the driveway.

'Fuck,' Kiri curses. He jumps out of the car, runs to it, and picks it up.

'Hurry up,' I urge, looking nervously towards the back of the house. Soon the guards and dogs will return.

'Come on, come on,' I say, my voice full of panic. I can already hear the dogs coming around the side of the house. They will tear Kiri to bits if they find him running in the compound. As he nears I put my foot on the pedal, and the car starts moving. The rest of the guards should be arriving soon. I pray they don't arrive early.

Kiri lunges into the open car door and slams it closed as I drive through the gates. Vasluv gets the gates to clang into place just as the dogs slam themselves against it in such a frenzy of barking that their mouths froth. In the rear mirror I see one of them running to where the shoe dropped, sniffing the ground at the scent left by Kiri.

My palms are sweating so much they slip on the steering wheel. I wipe them on my jeans one by one as I slowly drive down the road and pick up Vasluv. After driving around the block I park the car and call Baba.

10.59: 'Is it still okay?' I ask.

251

'Nothing to worry about, child. I've spoken to the guards. Apparently, it was just a false alarm. There was a glitch and the electricity went off. It's back on again and everybody is back at their stations.'

I breathe a sigh of relief and with shaking hands start the engine again.

Thirty-four

Tasha Evanoff

It is a strange, almost surreal feeling to know that I have defeated a ruthless Mafia gangster's security system, though to be fair to the gangster, I had an unfair advantage. One he never considered when he was setting up his security system. That he would be betrayed by his own family.

I think of my father sleeping like a baby in the trunk of the car while he takes his last journey on this earth, and don't feel the least bit frightened or regretful. In fact, I feel nothing. Not even anger in my heart. My father has already taken all that I loved away from me. I don't allow my mind to dwell on Noah even for a second. The loss is too great, too profound. I don't think I have started to come to terms with the idea that he might be gone, just like Sergei. Part of a dream.

No, I'd rather push it away and deal with it later when I am able to.

I focus my mind on the task at hand as we head to the outer rim of the city where I have only gone once. Then I was sixteen years old. I sat in the back of my father's car and paid careful attention as my father told me to learn the route by heart. This is the Evanoff safe house. Only he and I know of it. Not even Baba does.

'If ever there is any kind of trouble I want you to come here and wait until I come and get you.'

What a strange and twisted turn of fate that the very house that is meant to be a safe house for him and me, will end up as the most unsafe place for him.

It is dark and things don't look the same as they did in the bright light of day, but one by one the landmarks come into view, and one by one I tick them off. Bridge. Shell gas station. Vauxhall tube station. NCP carpark. Railway crossing. Weeping willow tree in the Seven-Eleven carpark. Block of Council estate apartments.

The men remain ducked. Almost an hour after we began our journey, I spot the row of industrial looking warehouse and mechanics. The area is badly lit and isolated. My father picked it because it is a place that you'd struggle to find without directions. It is also a place he is not known. A rough, depressed place where poor people live and work. We pass foraging foxes near some bins, a couple of beggars sleeping rough, and a group of kids drinking and smoking.

The roads are bad, filled with pot holes and I slow right down as I don't want to go past the entrance and have to double back. The more invisible we are the less attention we will attract. I peer worriedly out of the window. All these storefronts look so similar in the dark. Dimitri said the tranquilizer would keep my father out for up to three hours and since it's now been an hour-and-a-half since it was administered I'm anxious that we get him into the building and secured before he comes around.

'Here it is.' I announce with relief, as I spot the narrow doorway. I fish into my pocket for the key that he gave me, and take the small torch I brought.

I tell the men to wait in the car as I walk in the path of the headlights towards

the entrance door. The heavy lock looks rusted and I pray that the key will work. With a little persuasion the key goes in and thankfully turns. I have to use my shoulder to open the heavy door and then step inside. I shine my torch to the left and then the right, locate the light switches and pull them.

Yes!

Bravo Papa. You paid your bills.

The lights are not wonderful, but adequate and I start looking around for the door to the basement that he said was virtually soundproof. I spot it at the far end of the warehouse. The door is locked, but I find a key in my bunch and I open it. The air smells damp and stale. I shine my torch to the sides and find the light switch on the left of the door. I turn it on.

It's eerily silent. I take a few steps and nearly scream when something brushes my leg, Ugh, rats. Cobwebs catch my hair and send a shiver down my spine. Obviously no one has been here for a long time. I duck my head and see that the room itself is exactly as I remember it. There is a fridge a cupboard, a bed, chairs, tables. Everything you could possible need for a week's stay.

I go back outside and wave to the men to bring him in. While they are lifting my father from the trunk I reach for the rucksack that I placed in the car earlier in the evening.

I watch as they each take an arm from the inert man and wrap it over their shoulders. Then they rush him through the door. Once inside they let his sleeping body rest against a timber beam.

'What do you want us to do with him?' Kiri asks.

'Down here,' I call as I make my way down the short flight of steps. I turn around and watch them lie him on his back on the steps and simply let go. My father's body bumps all the way down. To be honest their roughness horrifies me and then I realize what a mad thought that is.

'Where next?' Kiri asks, standing next to my father's body. His voice is loud as it echoes and reverberates around us.

I scan the cold concrete room again. 'Put him on the chair and tie him up securely. The ropes are in the rucksack.' I point out.

'Okay Miss Evanoff.'

257

I look at my father as he sleeps on the chair and I am suddenly moved by his sleeping form. This is my father. What am I doing? I grasp my throat with my hand and remember what he did to Sergei. And my Noah. This is not my Papa. This man is a stranger. *Don't be fooled, Tasha. Behind that peaceful sleeping face lies the heart of an evil monster.*

'Are you sure he is properly secured? Hands and feet?' I ask.

'Yes, he can move his head so don't get too close to his face.' Vasluv the older man, tells me.

That brings a scatter of goosebumps on my flesh. I swallow my fear. 'Good,' I tell them. You can leave and I'll text you when it's time.'

'You'll be alright on your own?' Vasluv enquires.

I gaze at him blankly. I definitely did not expect concern from one of Dimitri's cold-blooded killers. 'Yes, yes, I'll be fine. Thank you.'

He nods. 'We will wait for your message to return and do the necessary.'

Thirty-five

Tasha Evanoff

My heart is in my throat as I watch them climb the steps and listen to their footsteps go along the upstairs warehouse floor, then I hear the door close behind them.

Alone in this depressing and creepy place, my plan seems outlandish, stupid even. Surely, I didn't think I could kill my own father. What was I thinking?

I should have asked one of them to do it.

I can still call them, but that would be the cowardly way out. I have to do it myself. I want my father to know why. I want to face him and let him know how he has hurt me with his actions. He never even gave Noah a chance. He just rubbed him out. Just like that. As if he was just a figment of my imagination. Now he'll never know how much I loved him. I feel myself choke up and, with a sniff, I turn away from the stairs, the door, the idea of letting someone else do my dirty work for me.

I pull a chair opposite my father and wait for him to wake up.

For nearly an hour I sit as if hypnotized and probably a little mad in front of him. Yes, mad with grief. When he opens his eyes I am meant to kill him. Who of my friends could imagine even in their wildest dreams little obedient, dutiful me sitting here contemplating murder? Yet, here I am. I must have become unhinged when I saw Sergei's body. I'm still unhinged.

The first sign that he is coming to makes my pulse hammer and my spine go ramrod straight. His eyes flicker and his mouth quivers. Soon his eyes open a little more, but he is still groggy and disoriented. He blinks and shakes his head. I think his mouth must be dry because he licks his lips and swallows. Perhaps they hurt his body too when they let him bump his way down the stairs because he winces.

His eyes widen when he tries to shake his body and finds that he cannot move. Suddenly, he becomes shockingly alert. His eyes narrow as they first fall on me, then look startled when he sees his environment. He looks down at the ropes that tether to the chair. He struggles, but only briefly, when the realization hits home that these are no amateur binds. He will not get free of them.

'What is going on Tasha? Why am I tied up? he demands.

'Try to guess, Papa.'

He frowns, suddenly remembering. 'You drugged me.' Then his voice changes. 'Who is here with you?' he demands.

'We're all alone Papa. Just you and me like all those times we went out to eat ice cream and we went to the movies together.'

'What nonsense are you talking about?' he asks harshly. All traces of sleep has fled from his eyes, and he is as furious as I have ever seen him. His face is red with it.

I shake my head. Even at a time like this my father will never give an inch.

'Who has put you up to this?' he demands.

'You did, Papa.'

He stares at me. 'What do you mean?'

'It's a good thing you asked, because I've been meaning to tell you anyway. I've never told you, have I, how hurt I was when you kicked mama out of the house and never let me see her. All those years you forced me to hide and lie and run around meeting Mama in toilets. You denied me a mother,' I scream.

Tears start filling my eyes and I dash them away.

'I forgave you all that, because I loved you. I pretended to myself that it's not as bad as all that. Then when I told you what a horrible man Oliver is you didn't care. You still wanted to sacrifice me to your ambition and greed for power and status.'

'What are you talking about? I told you I'd protect you from him,' he cuts in aggressively.

'Oh, Papa. You are such a liar. You knew even if he did terrible things to me I would never come and complain to you. I was too frightened of you. I would just bear it as I have borne everything else.'

'Look. This is silly. All right. You don't have to marry him. You have my word.'

'You think you're here because of *that*?'

The first flash of fear crosses his eyes. 'Then what?'

'You sent someone into my bedroom to kill Sergei. He was like my son, Papa. He was an innocent little thing and I loved him with all heart, and you just took him away. How could you? How could you?' I sob. The tears are rushing down my cheeks, and I'm ugly crying, but I don't care anymore.

'*Solnyshko* Sergei was not your son. Sergei was a dog. One day you will have a child and you will understand. You are my daughter, my flesh and blood. Everything I have done is for your own good. All of this we can put aside ... and start again. Maybe I've been too harsh with you. I'll change ... I'll be a better father. What do you say?' his voice is soft and manipulative.

'As if that wasn't enough you then took the only man I've ever wanted. I loved Noah, Papa. I would have given up my life for him. I didn't even get a chance to tell him. You took everything away from me.'

'*Solnyshko* listen to me,' he says, his voice is not sorry or remorseful. It is just wheedling. It's all just a technique. A trick. A bluff. As if I'm stupid.

For a few seconds I continue to stare at his pathetic attempt at finding a way out of his mess.

'You are young and beautiful. You will find someone else,' he says.

I walk over to where my rucksack is on the floor and feel his eyes follow. I kneel down, pull out the untraceable handgun I got from Dimitri's men, and take the safety catch off. I get to my feet and walk towards him with the gun in my hand. What irony that it was my father who taught me how to use a gun.

Thirty-six

Tasha Evanoff

If rain drops were kisses. I could send you showers. If hugs were seas. I'd send you oceans. If love was a person I'd send you me!

-Shahid Abbas

'**I**t's too late for that,' I say softly.

My heart feels like a piece of ice. 'You are a destructive rabid dog. The poison is in your bloodstream and the only humane thing to do is to put you down.'

He struggles instinctively, making the chair rock so violently on the concrete floor it almost topples over. Curiously, for I have become quite removed from the scene around me I see real uncontrollable fear slither into the bully's face. He's beginning to sweat. For the first time in our lives the power is in my hands.

Without warning he stops struggling and makes a great effort to control himself. He's changing tactics. He laughs. It has a harsh hollow sound to it.

'You think it is so easy to take a man's life. It doesn't end when you have pulled the trigger. Let me tell you about the nightmares. They come back. Their souls haunt you. There's nowhere to run. Kill me in cold blood, you want me in your nightmares, because I swear, Tasha, I will never forget this ingratitude. I will haunt you until your dying day and after you are dead I will be waiting for you in hell.'

My hand shakes and I use the other hand and try to keep it steady.

'Look at you. Shaking like a leaf. You're not a killer. You haven't got it in you. Just like that bitch who bore you. Weak. Go on. I dare you. Pull the trigger and see what happens after. It won't be unicorns shitting rainbows,' he taunts.

His words have a strange effect on me. They make me feel light-headed. I swallow back the strange sensation and try to stay focused.

'This is for Sergei and Noah,' I say, but my voice is weak and uncertain compared to his loud, aggressive threats and taunts.

'Stop this now, Tasha and I promise there will be no repercussions. I will put it down to temporary madness caused by grief over your dog. I give you my word here. You know me. I have never broken my word to you ever, have I?'

I bring the gun up to his chest height, with one finger on the trigger and the other tightly clasping my firing hand.

He changes strategy again 'For God's sake Tasha you can't shoot your father. What will your life be after this? Do you want this on your conscience?' he cries.

The more he talks the more confused I become.

I try to think of my poor Sergei, and Noah, and how much I hate my father, but it is not like in the movies. Pulling the trigger is difficult. Sweat prickles across my neck and my armpits are drenched. I straighten my body, point the gun, close my eyes, but I just can't hold the gun straight.

'You see Tasha, you're not a killer. Now listen to your Papa and untie me. Let's get away from here. We are family. What will Baba say if she knew what you have done? You will break her heart.' There is hope in his voice now and his face is no longer so fearful. He thinks he is stronger than me. He thinks he knows me. He knows which buttons to push. He can win this.

That is when I decide I *can* pull the trigger. I realize that I'm not doing this to be vindictive. I'm not even doing this for revenge. Sergei and Noah will not come back whether I take his life or not. I'm doing this because someone like him shouldn't be allowed to walk this earth. I don't need to tell him that Baba planned this together with me. Without her help I would never have been able to carry out this murder without getting caught.

Maybe he is right, I was so caught up in the planning that I'd lost sight of what it takes to actually kill someone. I suddenly find myself overcome by all the emotions and feel my resolve slipping.

'Think about what you are doing Tasha? Do you think there won't be an investigation? How many clues have you left behind? Do you want to spend the rest of your life in prison? They love blonde little girls like you in prison. You want to be someone's bitch? Is that what you want? There'll be no more trips to the hairdressers and shopping and holidays and forget about having a dog. The only dog around will be you. An ungrateful little bitch for all the tough, hardened criminals. You'll be eating pussy for the rest of your life. How about that, huh?'

Tears start running down my face. I take a big gulp of air. I can do this. I have to. No matter what happens after this I have to end it here and now, not only me, mama and Baba will get punished.

Cursing he bares he teeth at me. 'Enough is enough. Don't make me any more angry than I am already. I am your father. I order you to untie me right now,' he barks impatiently as if he is somehow controlling all around him. In that moment I look into his eyes and I know I cannot untie this man. He will not rest until his revenge is absolute. I know that I can and must do this. I train my gun on him again.

'I'm sorry, Papa. I can't do that. This is the end. No matter what happens to me after this you will not walk out of this room on your own two feet.

His face changes suddenly. He starts sobbing. I mean great big tears roll out of his eyes. What an actor my father is.

'I'm sorry, *Solnyshko*. I'm so sorry. You are right. I've been a terrible father. I beg of you. Please. Spare me. You are kind and good. This is not you. You are an angel. You could never shoot a helpless human being. I know you. You are kind and gentle. Remember that time you rescued the bee. Remember, you found him on the floor and you picked him and let him drink sugar water from the palm of your hand until he recovered and flew away. That's you. Not this. Tasha, you have taught me a great lesson that I will never forget. You've made me a better man.'

Oh, God. I can't. I just …. My hands are shaking so badly.

'Shut uuuuuuup,' I scream.

I will count to ten. I can do this. I have to. Ten, nine, eight, seven, six…. My hands are still trembling but a bit less. I put my finger on the trigger. I close my eyes.

'Pleeeeaseeee,' my father begs. This time it's real.

Tears and snot run down my face. My mouth is open in a silent cry as I start to depress the trigger.

'You're right, Nikita she can't, but I can.'

My eyes fly open, but the words have barely time to register in my dazed, confused brain before I see my father topple over with a small hole in his forehead. How quick and silent his death, but I didn't shoot Papa!

My head swings around and my mouth drops open in shock.

'You're ... alive!'

Thirty-seven

Jack Irish

Two Days Before

https://www.youtube.com/watch?v=vvv
X5QM4z3Y
Wicked Game

When I lean over the man, his hand instinctively reaches out to grip my wrist. He is dying in a narrow alleyway, but he is a fighter. There is still surprising strength in his grip.

'Who are you?' he asks.

'I'm a doctor.'

He lets go of my hand, and grips my shirt. 'Don't let them hurt her,' he whispers urgently.

Then his eyes dim and he starts to lose consciousness. I rip his blood soaked shirt open and see the gash. It's pretty bad. Blood is seeping out like a hot water spring. I also don't miss all the tattoos that immediately identify him as someone from the Russian mafia. As I press my hand to the wound, I see a man, dragging himself along the ground towards us. His face is contorted with pain and his leg is broken. Behind him I see more bodies on the floor, but they are not moving.

'It's not what you think it is,' he says. He has a lisp that makes him sound like he is hissing. 'Don't get involved. It is dangerous for you. My people are on their way. You better run, pretty boy, and quick if you want to stay pretty.'

I look at the unconscious man. He took them all down on his own. That means he's lethal, but if I don't do something to stop his wound from bleeding out he will die. I look at the creature dragging himself along the ground. The last thing I need in my life is to get involved in some Russian Mafia gang fight. My car is parked less than a few feet away. I can be identified by it, and they will come after me. I glance again at the man's wound. First rule of medicine: Do no harm.

Oh, fuck it.

I look at the guy slithering towards me. 'I suggest you stop right there. Don't come an inch closer.'

He stops and makes a strange sound. Presumably, he is cursing me in Russian. 'Are you stupid, boy? A whole team of men with knives and guns are on their way here. I have seen you and even if you kill me there is a security camera at the top of this street. They will identify you. They will come after you. You are a dead man walking. He is almost dead anyway.'

'Whatever. Stay right where you are, or I will have to kill you myself.'

His eyes bulge with incredulity. 'This man is nothing to you. You don't know him at all. Do you know he is a contract killer? He has killed many people. He is not a good man. You want to *kill* for him? Or worse give up your life for his?'

I look down at the wounded man. He does look dangerous, and I can well believe that he could be a contract killer. He has the eyes and physique for it, but even at the moment he believed himself to be dying his only concern was for saving a woman. I'll take my chances with him any day.

'You're making a big mistake,' the other guy says.

'Shut the fuck up.' I take my jacket off and rip my shirt off quickly.

'You are a fool. I promise you my men will arrive any moment now.'

'Another word out of you and my boot's going to end up your mouth.'

I tear my shirt into wide strips, and tie the strips together to make a long bandage. I look around at the walls of the alleyway. There is a black water pipe. I run to it. My guess was right. It is full of spider webs.

I take my credit card out of my wallet and as fast as I can, collect the spider's web behind the pipe in my hand. Then I run the edge of the credit card along my palm so that all the white strands end up on the card.

Getting on my haunches I press my credit card spider's web side facing his wound. Spider silk helps stop bleeding and speeds healing. I learned this little gem from an old African healer. Holding the credit card tight against the wound I tie the shirt-bandage firmly around his chest. I tear the ends and tie it up.

I feel his throat. His pulse is weak but steady.

I glance around. His mates have still not arrived. I might just make it. I cover the wounded man with my jacket and go and unlock my car. I open the passenger door and put the seat down. Running back to him I get behind him. Putting my hands under his armpits I carefully sit him upright. Then using my body as a wall to help support his weight, I stand, lifting him up with me. Once standing I take a deep breath.

He's a big guy and my next move has to be lightning fast.

Grasping his right hand and holding it at 90 degrees to his body, I duck under it, and pop up in front of him before he can collapse on me. Still holding his wrist I bend my knees and use the fireman's lift to get him on to my shoulders.

With him securely and mostly balanced over my right shoulder I jog as fast as I can to my car. I'm conscious that any moment the other guy's compatriots could turn up and I'm really not in the mood, or drunk enough, to take on a bunch of guys wielding knives and guns.

'You won't get away with this,' the guy on the ground threatens. There is a tinge of desperation to his voice. The guy is shit scared of the reaction of whoever ordered the hit.

As I lay the man in the front seat, sweat is dripping off my body, even though it is a cold mid-October night. I close the door and jump into the front seat. As I am driving out of the street I see the thugs drive into the road in a blacked out black Merc.

I knew instantly it was them because one of them has his glass down and his elbow is resting on the edge of the window. A blind man couldn't miss those tattoos. As our cars pass I look in and see them. You can tell they are thugs from a mile away – they have hard mean faces and they look pissed as hell.

Well done, Jack. You just fucking missed them by seconds.

Thirty-eight

Noah Abramovich

Present Time

https://www.youtube.com/watch?v=lDp
njE1LUvE
Where The Wild Roses Grow

Frozen, she stares at me, her eyes bigger than I've ever seen them. So vulnerable. So childlike. And one step away from a murderer. If I'd waited one more second she would have pulled the trigger and the loveliest, purest human being I know would have been tainted with blood forever. In a daze she wipes her nose with the back of her hand.

'I would have done it,' she says in a strange whisper.

'That sin is not for you,' I say.

Her lips quiver. 'But it shouldn't be on you.'

I smile. 'If I have to go to hell for anything let it be this.'

Fresh tears fill her eyes and start running down white cheeks. 'If you're going to hell then that's where I'm going too,' she sobs.

'You won't like it. It's hot down there and the Devil lied when he said they have ice cream.'

Her eyes roam my body restlessly. She is still in shock. 'I thought you were dead.'

'I thought I'd stay around for a bit longer. See what setting up house with you will be like. Maybe move to Nice. Maybe have a couple of kids.'

She tries to smile, but the emotions pouring through her are too much and it comes out like a grimace. She sways as if she is about to faint, and I lunge to catch her. The movement makes my ribs fucking sing. Fuck. I feel sweat break out on my forehead as I hold her trembling body. Her hands grasp my jacket fearfully, and her eyes look at me anxiously.

'Oh! My God! You're hurt,' she cries pulling herself away. The panic in my voice echoes around the room.

'It's nothing,' I brush off.

She reaches for the zip of my jacket and pulls it open. Hers hands fly to her mouth. 'Oh, God, you're bleeding through the bandages' she exclaims, staring at blood soaked mess of my bandages. I must have opened the wound in my rush to get here.

'What the hell Noah?'

'Hey, it's not as bad as it looks. I just need some fresh bandaging and I'll be fine.' I say in a calm voice.

As I watch, the delicate hot-house flower becomes that single scarlet rose growing wild amongst rock, daring men to brave her thorns and take her. I watch the transformation with awe. This woman never stops surprising me.

'No, you're not fine Noah, you're losing blood. No wonder you're so pale. We need to get you to a hospital.'

'I'm not going to a hospital. I have a doctor waiting to attend to me.'

'How did you get here?'

'I drove.'

She nods distractedly. Her mind figuring something out. She tilts her head back. 'How did you find me?'

'You gave the address to your grandmother. I called her.'

She nods again, frowning. 'You're not staying at your house, are you?'

'No.'

'Are you somewhere safe?'

'Very. I'm staying with some Irish gypsies.'

'Irish gypsies?'

'It's a long story. I'll tell you all about it when we have the time.'

'Fair enough. Will you be able to drive yourself back?'

'Tasha. Stop right there. I'm not going anywhere without you. I'm staying right here. I'm calling some people. First thing we have to do is get rid of him, then get you back to the house with a credible story.'

She shakes her head. 'No need. I've already made all the arrangements and I've got my story ready.'

'You have?' I stare at her with surprise.

'You don't rob a bank without a getaway plan,' she says.

I smile, impressed and proud of her. 'No you don't. Tell me the plan.'

'All right. First of all, I went to see Dimitri Semenov.'

I whistle with admiration. Dimitri Semenov. Her father's most bitter enemy. He must have been cumming in his pants. When Tasha decides to do something she doesn't do it in halves.'

'He gave me two of his men. They helped me bring pa ... him here and they are going to dispose of the car and body. All I have to do now is call them. I was going to get them to drop me off at a minicab company in town but now that you are here you can do it.'

I frown. 'Okay, so they get rid of the body and the car. What happens then?'

'I wear a black wig. You drop me off at the first minicab company we come across. I then tell the taxi driver to drop me off two blocks away from my house. I jog to my house and call my grandma. She throws the rope ladder over the fence. I climb it and get into the house and pretend I've been in bed all night. Tomorrow morning when the household discovers my father is missing we'll call the police.

I frown. 'Didn't your father install one of the best security systems with cameras all around the house and four guards day and night. How did you dodge the guards? And wouldn't the cameras have caught you driving out in your father's car?'

She explains exactly how Baba, Kiri and Vasluv did it.

To be honest, I'm impressed. Not bad at all for a little girl who never said boo to anyone in her life, but I still have to quiz her about the most important thing. 'What will you tell the police tomorrow?'

'I'll tell them Papa went to bed after dinner and that was the last I saw of him. I sleep deeply and never heard a thing.'

'You're sure you're not on any of the video?'

'One hundred percent.'

I look closely at her then at the dead man on the plastic tarp. Can she really pull this off? 'What if there are cameras in the streets that have recorded your journey here?'

'I went to the garage and changed the plates earlier this evening.'

'What about the phone calls you've been making tonight?'

'Pay as you go mobile and I'm dumping it later this morning in other people's bins.

I nod with approval.

'Don't worry, Noah. I have planned this very carefully.'

'I can make it easier for you. I can arrange a fake kidnapping attempt. This way it won't look like such an inside job.'

'No,' she says and her voice is very sure and calm. 'I don't want anyone else to take the blame for this. In fact, I am very sad that I was too gutless to pull the trigger, and that you were the one who had to do it. I don't want you to go to a different place than me. If you're going to hell, I want to go there too, ice cream or no ice cream.'

'Fine. Shall we get the ball rolling?'

She fishes her mobile from her pocket and hits a button. 'It's done,' she says into it. Then she closes it and looks at me. 'I've so many questions for you, but they can wait. However, there is something very important I have to say to you now.' She stops to clear her throat.

'Go on,' I encourage.

'If something goes wrong tonight and for some reason I don't make it, I want

284

you to know that I love you, Noah. I love you more than life itself.

I hold her beautiful face between my palms. 'Nothing will happen to you. I'm not trusting you to any minicab driver. I'll call Sam and ask him to meet us somewhere. He will drive you to the end of your road and wait until he has seen you climb the ladder.

A single tear flows from one of her eyes. I wipe it away. 'And just in case anything happens to me and I don't make it, I want you to know that I love you, Tasha. I love you like I've never loved anyone in my whole life. I'd die for you, girl.'

Thirty-nine

Tasha Evanoff

https://www.youtube.com/watch?v=-n-2lPzH7D0
Anak

I put the rope ladder away and go into the kitchen. Baba is sitting in front of her customary pot of tea. Her face is pale and sadder than I have ever seen it.

'Is he ... gone?'

I nod.

She closes her eyes and swallows violently as she tries to regain control of her emotions.

I kneel beside her and cover her clenched fist with my hand. Even though I'm the one who was out in the cold all night, her hands are freezing.

She opens her eyes and nods. 'You did well, my child. You did well.' Her voice breaks on the last word and I throw my arms around her neck.

'It wasn't me. I was too cowardly. I couldn't pull the trigger.'

A ghost of a smile appears on her lips. 'I'm glad it wasn't you. A child shouldn't have to kill her own father, even if he is a monster.'

'Noah did it.'

Her eyes widen. 'He's alive?'

'Yes.' I say with a nod. 'He's wounded, but he's alive.'

'Where is he now?'

'I don't know the full details, but it's some kind of a safe house run by Irish gypsies.'

She nods distractedly. 'Where is your father now?'

'They've taken his body away.'

Her lips press down so hard they are a thin straight line. 'To be disposed of how?'

'I don't know. I didn't ask, but it has to be in such a way that it is never found.' I don't tell her about the pig farm and greedy pigs.

She looks down at the floor. 'Did he ... suffer?'

'No. It was instant. One bullet.'

'Was he angry with me?'

I stroke her hair. 'He died not knowing you helped me.'

A great sob racks her body. It comes from her very core and makes her hands tremble so uncontrollably I become scared.

'Oh, Baba,' I cry helplessly. 'Don't cry so hard. Please. You'll become ill.'

She makes a great effort to calm herself, but tears flow down her cheek ceaselessly.

'I'm sorry, Baba. I made you choose between him and me.'

'You didn't, my child. I made that choice myself.'

'I wish there could have been another way.'

'There wasn't. Don't you think if there was I wouldn't have taken it? He was my son, my flesh and blood. I carried him in my belly for nine months. Nine months. I never told you that when he was born he was small and sickly, always crying with colic. He would cry for hours and his father would get so annoyed, sometimes I'd wrap him up tightly and take him out to the garden in the middle of the night. I'd sit for hours in the cold just rocking him until he was so exhausted with crying he fell asleep.'

She sniffs.

'Then I'd try to get up and find my legs were so cold they wouldn't work. When he was four he got inflammation of the cornea and the doctor said he could become blind. I took him to the church every day. I fell on my knees and prayed for him to be able to see again. When he was older and he went into this life I got on my knees again to beg forgiveness for the terrible things he was doing. I asked that his heart be shown the path to repentance. Most of my life I've been praying for him, but I never felt any of it was a sacrifice. I loved him so much. He was my life, my heart, my soul.'

'I'm so sorry, Baba.'

She smiles sadly. 'Once when he was only a boy and he was being naughty I told him, "Do you know I carried you in my belly for nine months and this is how you repay me?" You know what he said?'

I shake my head.

'He said, "Tell me how much rent you want for those nine months and I'll pay it. This way I won't have to listen to you going on about how you carried me in your stomach for the rest of my life." He was only seven-and-a-half years old then, but I should have known that day. A child who shows no gratitude is not going to turn out well.'

I look at her sadly. It is impossible to comfort her. Her love is deeper than I realized.

'What will happen now?' she asks.

'I will lodge a police report that Papa is missing. We will all, including Mama, help the investigators with all their queries, but as none of us knows anything we won't be able to help much.'

'What about this house and the servants?' she asks.

'Of course we will continue to live in this house for a while. Then, I will move out and go to live with Noah, and after a couple of months you will come to live with me. I don't want any of Papa's wealth so I won't be declaring him dead. Let the lawyers sort it out in time.'

'Have you eaten, Baba?' I ask.

'No. I'm not hungry.'

'I heard you being sick in the bathroom when you went up to your room.'

'Yes,' she admits. 'I threw up everything I ate last night.'

'I'm going to make some dried mushroom and barley soup and you're going to try to eat some, alright?'

She nods.

'I'll be back.' First I take the battery out of my mobile phone. I'll throw the pieces away later. Then I go into the larder to find the ingredients. As I start to prepare the soup Baba comes to me and helps me.

I smile at her as we cook together, filling the kitchen with warm smells from Baba's past.

Forty

Tasha Evanoff

After I have fed Baba and helped her back to her room, I square my shoulders and go to my father's room. His room is big and strangely still. The shutters are closed and it is dark. For a moment I stand at the doorway and feel a sensation of remorse. I took a man's life. Even if I did not pull the trigger, it was I who orchestrated him into that position, and would have eventually pulled the trigger. I was a hair's breadth away.

My father was right. I will never be the same again.

Then I shake off the dark sense of disquiet and switch on the light.

His bed is crumpled and clearly shows the marks of his body being pulled out of it. I have to be out of here before the servants start arriving. I pull on my rubber gloves, walk to the bed, and rearrange it so it looks the way it would if someone got out of it naturally.

Then I collect his wallet, his belt, his money clip, and his shoes, and put them all into a laundry bag. I take one last look then I switch off the light and go to my own room. I add my clothes and shoes to my father's things and lock the laundry bag in my safe. I will burn everything later.

Then I go into the shower.

While I am standing in the strong cascade of warm water I have a strange sensation. As if what is happening to me can't be real. My father is dead. Sergei is dead. Noah told me he loves me. My grandmother is completely devastated. Noah is alive. I'm a murderer.

After my shower I go downstairs to the kitchen.

'Where's Rosita?' I ask the chef.

'I think she's in the laundry room,' he says.

I run down to the basement and find her folding some sheets.

She smiles broadly. 'You're up early.'

'No, I'm not,' I deny guiltily, then I stop myself. 'Yeah, I drank a lot last night and slept like a log. I woke up with a headache, but thank God it's gone now that I've had a shower.'

Rosita smiles politely while she waits to hear what I want from her.

'Hey, you know the puppy I gave you the other day, where is it now?'

Her smile suddenly widens to a big, toothy, grin.

'Come, come. It is good that you have come to take him. He's very naughty. Impossible to work when he is around,' she says, and takes me to the corridor.

Just outside the cellar door is a cage with the poor puppy inside it. He is sitting upright and staring at us curiously. I open the cage door and take him into my arms. He is ecstatic to be out of the cage and licks my face with his tiny little tongue.

'I'm so sorry. It's not your fault at all. You're a good little boy,' I say kissing his soft ears.

Then I take him with me upstairs to Baba's room.

He'll never take Sergei's place, but he deserves better than being locked up in a cage in the basement. One day I'll learn to love him.

I put him on the floor in Baba's room. He starts running around like a mad thing. Just like Sergei used to.

I look at Baba. 'If you don't mind, I'm going to call him Niki. He will be Papa's gift to us. He will be one of the good things that Papa gave to me.'

I wait until 2.00pm when it has become certain among the servants and everybody in the household that Papa is missing. Something is wrong. Then I call Oliver. He doesn't pick up and I am about to leave a message when he comes on.

'Hello Tasha,' he says. How I could have thought I could marry him or live with him seems incredible now. I must have been a different person. Not truly living at all.

'Oliver, I'm calling to give you the bad news that my father is missing.'

'What do you mean missing?'

'He left in his car in the middle of the night and now neither he nor his car can be found.'

'Are you joking?'

'Of course not,' I say coldly.

'Sorry,' he apologizes, taken aback by my coldness. 'It just seems so incredible.'

'Anyway, the reason I'm calling is to tell you under the circumstances there won't be a wedding.'

'Not so fast. Your father and I had a deal.'

'Yes, I know. You'll have to take it up with him when he shows up.'

'Goodbye.'

'Hang on a minu—'

I end the call. 'That's that,' I say, and a smile comes to my lips.

My phone rings. It is him. I reject the call and block his number.

It is time to go to the police. I buy a new pay as you go, throw my old cell phone in a bin on Park Lane and the battery in a bin outside the police station just before I go in to make a missing person report.

That night I sleep in Baba's room with Niki.

Forty-one

Jake Eden

You could have knocked me down with a feather when my brother Shane called while on holiday in Guyana. He told me he needed a safe house for a man hiding from the Russian Mafia.

'You better not be fucking involved with the Russian Mob,' was my first reaction.

He assured me he was not.

My next was question. 'How the fuck do you know anyone who needs a safe house?'

'It's a long story,' he says. He doesn't want to say it on the phone. Long story short. He owed a favor to Zane, the Russian mobster who became Alexander Malenkov, the world famous pianist. I had no idea Shane even knew Zane. Sometimes Shane surprises me. All my life I always treated him as a kid. The playboy of the family, but when the chips are down he always surprises me.

The man's name is Noah Abramovich and, by the way, he's injured. So I arranged for him to be collected from this doctor's apartment and transferred to the safe house. This afternoon I'm supposed to pick up Tasha Evanoff and take her to him. I know her father rather well, actually. Corrupt as hell. His legitimate companies are a front for his shady businesses.

Tasha Evanoff and I agree to meet at Starbucks in Knightsbridge. I arrive five minutes before our appointed time, but she is already there. I recognize her straightaway. Butter-wouldn't-melt-in-her-mouth, a blue-eyed blonde Russian beauty with an inner core of pure steel.

She's the opposite of my wife. My Lily looks tough on the outside, but she's delicate inside. Sometime when I look at her, I feel a twinge of worry. I'll stand at the window watching her feeding her birds and she seems so far away, so unreachable that it makes me want to run down the stairs, grab her tight and fuck her so I'm inside her, I'm part of her.

So that there's nothing else in her head and mind except me. It makes me fiercely protective. Ever since we got together I haven't left her alone for a single night. I take her everywhere with me. If she can't come, I don't go. I don't trust anyone else with her. No. Better safe than sorry.

'Tasha Evanoff?'

'Hello, Mr. Eden. Thank you for taking me to see him.' Her accent is pure upper-class, the best that money can buy. She stands, even though the finishing schools she must have attended would have told her it was not necessary, and extends her hand. She is dressed in an expensively understated and very conservative blue top and skirt, but there're a lot of secrets going on behind those wary eyes.

I take her hand. She has never done a day's work in her life. 'Jake Eden. No need to thank me. It's a pleasure,' I say.

She bites her bottom lip. 'Is he alright?'

'Other than suffering from a broken heart, yeah.'

She smiles.

'That's better.' I look down at the table. She has nearly finished her latte.

'Would you like something to drink?' she asks.

'Actually, no. I'm parked on double yellow lines.'

She picks up her purse and follows me out. There is no ticket on the windscreen. I open the passenger door and help her get in. She picks a toy from between her feet.

'You have children?'

I smile. 'Three.'

'That's nice.'

'Yes, it is.'

I start the engine and my phone rings. 'That's my oldest one, Liliana calling now.' I put her on speaker and edge into traffic.

'Daddy. You won't believe what Tommy has done,' she says furiously.

'What has he done?'

'He's put a bucket of sand down my toilet and now it's stuck.'

'What did you do to him first?'

'Nothing.'

'Are you sure about that?'

'Well, he started it.'

Tasha giggles.

300

'Who's that with you?' she asks instantly.

'You don't know her,' I say.

'How do you know? I might,' she says impertinently.

Tasha laughs again.

'Does mummy know her?'

'No, mummy doesn't know her.'

'Does she go to my school?'

'Liliana, you don't know her. Now can we get back to your problem with Tommy?'

'But how do you know I don't know her. I know lots of people. You should let me talk to her, Daddy,' she says confidently in that adult voice that freaks most people out.

By now Tasha can't stop giggling.

I look at Tasha. 'Do you want to speak to my daughter?'

As I get on the M25 my daughter is busy thoroughly interrogating the daughter of one of London's hidden Russian Mafia bosses. Fifteen minutes later and the conversation is still going strong.

'You should come to our house,' my daughter says. 'You'll like it here. We have a big dog, and a small cat, many fishes, two naughty hamsters and lots of birds. You can stay in the guest room. Do you want to come?'

'Well, thank you. Maybe I'll come around one day.'

'Come this, Friday,' Liliana invites.

'Er … maybe not this Friday,' Tasha says.

'What about Saturday?' my daughter insists.

'Liliana. How many times must I tell you not to force people to do things they don't want to.'

'I'm not forcing Tasha. She said she wanted to come.'

'Anyway,' I say. 'Tasha has to go now. Say goodbye.'

'Bye Tasha. Daddy, about Tommy …'

'Liliana, I'm just about to arrive. Can we discuss this a bit later?'

'Oh, all right,' she huffs.

'Good girl.'

'Love you,' she says.

'See you later.'

'Say it back,' she demands.

'I love you, pumpkin.'

'Bye Daddy,' she sings happily before the line goes dead.

'What an awesome kid,' Tasha says wishfully.

'Try living with that 24 seven,' I say, but in actual fact, I burst with pride when I think of her.

'I'd love a kid like that,' Tasha says. 'She's so intelligent and so alive.'

I smile. 'Yes, she is that.'

I turn off at the Chertsey turning and after a few roads we turn into a dirt lane with fields on either side of the road. Suddenly a man appears as if out of nowhere on the road. He doesn't move. Other men appear. They surround the car. I feel the energy in the car change. Their fierce, unkempt appearance and their unsmiling faces make Tasha nervous.

'Who are these people?' she asks.

'They're my people. Irish gypsies.'

She turns towards me. Her eyes are full of fear. 'You trust them?'

I look her in the eye. 'With my life.'

She exhales and I feel the tension drain out of her body.

I wind down the window.

One of the men lays his boxer's arm on the top of the car and leans in. He smells of bacon and beer. 'How's it going, Craig?' I ask.

His sparkling blue eyes crinkle at the corners. 'Mornin' to ya, Jake, m'boy. No news is good news.'

Forty-two

Tasha Evanoff

After Jake and the man exchanged a few words in a dialect so thick I barely could make out a few words, the crowd of intimidating, dirty, staring people, who I assumed must be the inhabitants of the caravans in the fields on either side of us, part to allow the car through.

The car comes to a stop in front of a plain bungalow with a red roof. Noah is sitting outside smoking a cigarette. To my great relief he looks well. When he sees the car he flicks away his cigarette and comes up to us as we get out of the car.

'I'll be having a beer with the boys, but I'll be back to pick her up in an hour,' Jake says as he closes his door.

'Thanks,' Noah says.

'No problem,' he throws over his shoulder, his long, muscular legs already walking away.

I stand there, my chin slightly dipped, looking at Noah. In the cold light of the day I feel suddenly shy. A weak autumn sun struggles out from under grey clouds and shines down on us. He crooks his finger at me.

I pretend to look around, then raise my eyebrows, and point to my chest.

Grinning he nods.

God, I love him so much. I run to him, my heart so stuffed with love it feels like it will burst. He takes my hand and twirls me around. 'How come you're more beautiful every time I see you?'

I grin like some kind of fool, and he gathers me in his arms and kisses me. Right there on the concrete driveway. A long slow burning kiss that just goes on and on.

Oh, Noah, Noah, Noah.

By the time he lifts his head, my cheeks are hot, and my lips are tingling.

'I love you,' I whisper.

'I'd burn everything I own down to the ground for you.'

'I've burnt everything I own to the ground for you,' I say.

He caresses my face with his thumbs. 'I want to wake up with a kiss like that every morning,' he says.

'Really?'

'Yeah, really. Can you do that?'

I nod.

'Good. I'll hold you to that.'

'Tell me,' I say with a flirtatious grin. 'When did you first know you loved me?'

'Hard to say. I wanted you for so long, the lines are blurred.'

'What kind of boring answer is that?' I complain. I can't tell my grandchildren that. Make up something better.'

'All right. I loved you before I was born, but I was forced to forget you because the pain of not having you was too unbearable, but all that time I knew that you were out there waiting for me. Many summers ago I saw you lying by the pool and I thought it was you, but I couldn't be sure. Until the day you showed up in a pink cardigan and I knew, my magic had returned.'

I gasp. 'That's beautiful.'

'I have so much to tell and find out from you, but I'm dying to fuck you,' he groans.

'What makes you think I'm not?' I ask cheekily.

He laughs and takes me into the bungalow. It's basic inside with cheap furniture and two rooms leading off from the hallway. Through one of the open doors I can see the bedroom with an unmade bed.

I look deep into his eyes. 'We'll have to be very careful. I don't want to hurt you.'

'Fuck being careful. That's for the others. Not us. Now will you take that dress off before I go mad.'

With a grin I unzip my dress and let it fall to the ground. Underneath I have on a skin-tight nurse's outfit and garters. His eyes widen.

'Well, well,' he says softly.

'Are you staring at me, Mr. Abramovich?'

'I'm always staring at you, Beautiful,' he purrs, his eyes swirling with appreciation and hot desire.

I flutter my eyelashes. 'So you don't think I look too slutty?'

'Never.'

I lick my lips lusciously. 'You're not just saying that?'

 308

He shakes his head. 'Nope.'

'You're too kind Mr. Abramovich.'

'Actually, I'm not feeling particularly kind right now.'

I take his hand and lead him into the bedroom. I go to the bed and pretend to plump the pillows, bending from the waist to reach for them, so he can see my naked bottom. I turn around and his face is a picture.

'Come and lie down on the bed so I can take your temperature. You may have a fever,' I say.

'Yeah, let's call it a fever.'

'Now come over here quickly. The doctor will be here soon. I don't want to lose my license to practice over this ... episode. You won't tell anyone will you?'

'Nope.'

'Oh good. It's very important that us nurses keep our reputations pure. If not, every Tom, Dick and Harry will be wanting a little extra, if you know what I mean.'

'Don't worry. I totally understand,' he says.

He walks over to the bed and lies down on it.

I get on the bed and start unzipping his pants.

'I thought you were going to take my temperature,' he says with just a hint of amusement in his voice.

I look at him sternly. 'Give me a minute. I'm just about to.'

His cock is as hard as a rock and it springs up when I release it. Wrapping my fingers around it, they look very feminine and white against the blood engorged hardness of his shaft, I smile mischievously at him. 'Hot and hard, I'm afraid.'

'I'm glad you figured that one out, Nurse Evanoff.'

'Are you being unnecessarily cheeky, Mr. Abramovich?'

He shakes his head.

I touch his balls. 'Do they feel tight and achy?'

'They do,' he agrees solemnly.

'I thought so.'

I bend down and plant a gentle kiss on his cockhead. His cock twitches in response. I take him in my mouth and slide my lips slowly down the smooth hot shaft while he groans with pleasure. Sucking him hard I pull my mouth away with a slurping sound. Then I lift my head.

'Mr. Abramovich, have you ever done it with a nurse before?' I ask, my voice all sultry and breathy.

'No,' he admits.

'Have you ever wanted to?'

'Mmmm ... it wasn't a great priority ... until today.'

I yank my dress until it is bunched up around my waist. Then I spread open my legs, and watch him stare at my freshly shaven pussy, with my clit poking out of its wet slit, and begging, just begging, to be fucked. Sitting down in his lap, I slide my pussy lips against his thick shaft.

'Do our bits joined together look like a hotdog, Mr. Abramovich?' I ask cheekily as I carry on running my crack up and down his hard dick.

'Oh fuck,' he swears, and tries to catch my waist and put me on his cock, but I slap his hands away.

'Patience, Mr. Abramovich. We have to be careful how we go about this.'

Soon my slit begins to slop against him and I can tell by his face that he is getting to the end of his tolerance. I rise up over him and inch by inch I impale myself on his shaft. Just a few days without him has been like forever to my body. I feel him stretch me and fill me completely. It feels so damn good I lay my palms on either side of him, and throwing my head back, ride him hard and deep, working up a sweat. I don't stop until my whole body starts to shake with my impending climax.

Sensing how close I am, he grabs hold of my bottom and pulls me more tightly against him, and more violently than can be good for his wound, thrusts upwards to squirt his seed as deeply inside me as he can. It seems as if it is ages that his cock spurts and spits inside me.

Panting, I grin at him. 'Do you feel any better, Mr. Abramovich?'

'Miles,' he murmurs, and pulling my body closer he kisses me deeply.

'I love you, Nurse Evanoff. I really, really, really fucking love you.'

'Well,' I breathe. 'I have to say, you are my best patient, Mr. Abramovich.'

'There better not be any other or you'll be dressing up as a morgue attendant soon.'

'It was always you for me,' I whisper.

Then I curl up against the unhurt side of his body and we talk. I tell him everything that has happened from the devastating moment I found Sergei, and he tells me about the doctor who found him on the street half dead. About the favor that Jake Eden's brother owed to Alexander Malenkov. Finally he tells me what his men have heard on the streets about my father's disappearance.

'What are they saying?'

'That Evanoff's daughter was seen at Dimitri Semenov's nightclub the day before he disappeared, but they have nothing else. No one knows anything.'

Then it is time for me to get dressed again.

Forty-three

Jack Irish

One Week Later

I look out of my window to the street below and I see the man dressed in a black leather jacket and black pants leaning against the lamp post across the street, smoking a cigarette.

The ground at his feet is littered with cigarette butts. I shrug into my jacket, stick my knife into the back of my jeans, and I go back to the window. He is still there looking as if hasn't a care in the world, but his eyes are sharp and alert.

I go down to the foyer, out into the crisp morning air and cross the street. He straightens from his leaning position and flicks his cigarette away. He smiles showing nicotine stained teeth. His hands are full of tattoos. He opens his box of Marlboro red and offers it to me.

'That stuff will kill you,' I say.

'It'll be a great thing if it's cigarettes that take me,' he says, his voice is whiskey-or-rather-vodka gravelly, and his accent makes him sound like he just got off the boat from Russia.

'What are you still doing here?'

He shrugs 'Just admiring the view.'

'Oh yeah?'

'Yeah, it's beautiful around here. Boss sends his regards by the way.'

I sigh. 'I thought the danger was past,' I say.

He grins. 'When you smash the head sometimes the tail jumps around for a bit.'

'Right. Tell your boss I don't want to see anybody hanging around here after today. We're quits. I did what was right and he owes me nothing,' I say, as I turn away.

'It's good to have friends. Maybe one day you need his help, da?'

I turn back and feel the knife dig into my back. 'Maybe never.'

'Never is a long time, Mr. Irish.'

315

Forty-four

Tasha Evanoff
One Month Later

A man slides into the seat in front of me.

I glance up and showing no change to my expression and take a sip of my latte. 'Hello, Inspector Stone,' I say.

He smiles. He has a pleasant smile. I've wondered about him. If he has a wife and children. What he's like when he is not facing someone he believes is a murder suspect.

'You've been shopping I see,' he says.

I was out shopping for a birthday present for Baba, but I'm damned if I'm going to give him an account of my shopping habits. It's got absolutely nothing to do with him, or his investigation. I look at him steadily and without any reaction.

'Is the food in this place any good?' he asks.

'I wouldn't be here otherwise.'

A waitress comes by with a menu. He takes the menu but doesn't open it. 'What's good here?' he asks her.

She shrugs and smiles. 'I'm a vegetarian, but I hear it's all good.'

'Can I have a burger?'

'We don't really do burgers,' she says with another smile, but slightly more forced this time. 'Have a look at our menu.'

'What about a cheese sandwich?'

If she could roll her eyes and not lose her job she would have. 'No, we don't do that here either.'

'Pasta?'

She looks at me as if for help or for some kind of female solidarity, but I can't help her. I'm down for worse than just exasperation. I fork another potato and put it into my mouth.

'Um ... we mostly just do Russian food. It *is* a Russian café.'

'What's she eating?' he asks, jerking his head in my direction.

'Red potato salad,' she says, glancing at my plate.

'Hmmm ... Nah. Bring me something closest to a burger, or a cheese sandwich, or even a good pasta.'

'How about meat dumplings?'

'Is that more like a burger or a cheese sandwich.'

The girl starts to look irritated. She turns to look meaningfully at the other tables that need her attention too. 'It's more like a meat filled pasta.'

He grins innocently. 'Great. That's what I'll have.'

'And what would you like to drink, Sir?'

'I'll have a Coke.'

'Thank you. I'll be back with it.' She escapes quickly.

I put my fork down, wipe my mouth and look up to find him watching me. He has watery gray eyes, and he blinks very often. I have a strong feeling that underneath this Columbo type bumbling exterior he affects, he is actually very sharp and intelligent.

'Your father's disappearance into thin air is a funny, funny case,' he says picking up the salt shaker and looking at the bottom of it as if there is something of vital importance there.

'Really? Why's that?'

'Mostly because it just doesn't make sense.'

'Oh?'

He spears me with those watery eyes. 'Unless it was an inside job.'

'That's an interesting idea.'

'Yes, I think so. For instance, all the security cameras were running perfectly except for camera 9.' He scratches his face, the pulls out a little notebook. He opens it and flicks to a page. 'It stops rotating from 10.24pm to 10.33pm. At first I thought it was glitch, but when I checked the camera I found some of paint had been chipped off the sides of it. As if, you know, someone had jammed a stick, or a piece of wood to keep it from swinging around.'

I look at him with interest.

'And the other thing is your grandmother got a call at, 'he refers to his notebook, 10.58pm from a pay-as-you-go mobile. A bit of a strange timing, wouldn't you say?'

'Did you ask her who it was?'

He smiles. 'Wrong number.'

I smile back. 'There you go then.'

'There is another anomaly. Your grandmother's call logs show that the only person she normally gets calls from is you, but on that night she received a call from a gentleman named Noah Abramovich at about 11.30pm. Yes, she claimed he hit the wrong button. Then she got another call at 2am from the same pay as you go number from earlier. Another wrong number. What are the odds of that happening?'

'Well, the odds of being hit by lightning in one's lifetime is millions to one and yet there are people who have been hit by lightning more than once and survived to tell the tale. I think there is a guy in the U.S. who has been hit six times.' I smile. 'We live in a weird and wonderful world, Inspector.'

He looks pained.

I affect a concerned expression. 'Surely you don't think my grandmother had anything to do with my father's disappearance?'

He ignores my question. 'Aren't you the sole heir of your father's estate?'

'I have no idea, and since I don't believe my father is dead but is simply missing, we won't know the contents of his will until either his body turns up, or the seven statutory years to get a declaration of presumed death is up.'

He leans forward. 'Why are you so eager to believe your father is missing and not dead?'

'I am his daughter. I prefer to believe that he is still alive and well somewhere. Is that so hard to understand Mr. Stone?'

His Coke arrives. He grabs the straw between his lips and sips at it in a desultory fashion. It makes me almost feel sorry for him.

I gather my purse and my bags. 'I should be going, but you will let me know if you find out anything at all, won't you, Inspector?'

He smiles cynically. 'You betcha.'

'Well, I'll wish you a good day then.'

'And you'll let me know if you find out anything at all, won't you, Miss Evanoff.'

'Of course. I'm just as eager to find my father as you are.'

He smiles. 'One day, Miss Evanoff. One day you'll make a mistake.'

I stand and smile slowly. He has no dead body and never will. He has nothing. 'I believe in karma. If I have done anything wrong, then I will pay the full price.'

'Good luck.'

'Thank you and the same to you.' I walk away, knowing his eyes are on me and feeling no fear.

Forty-five

Tasha Abramovich

Ten Months Later

https://www.youtube.com/watch?v=tB5
4XUhA9_w
My First My Last My Everything

The nurse puts the tiny little body in my hands. I hold that tiny little life that I have created in my body and I am filled with a fierce love. Death and damnation to anyone who hurts a hair on his tiny head. As dictated by custom Baba refused to let me talk about the name for the child. 'It will bring the evil eye. Tell no one.' Today is the first day I will be saying the name I have chosen for my son.

'Oh, look how red you are, Sergei?' I whisper. Not a day has gone by that I didn't think, talk, or pray for my Sergei. He was ripped away from me too soon.

Today I will do him the honor of naming my first born after him.

Sergei makes a tiny sound as he if he recognizes his name.

The door bursts open and Noah rushes in. He stops after two steps into the room. He looks pale. His hair is mussed and his eyes are quite wild. 'It's all over. The baby is out. Are you all right?' he asks urgently, his words running into each other.

'I'm alright and it is all over,' I say gently.

His face is a picture of guilt. 'I missed it all.'

'How's your head?' I ask holding back the laughter.

'It's alright,' he replies sheepishly

I grin at him and pretend to snort. 'Hrrmph ... Big mafia hero. Hired killer. Faints at the first sight of blood.'

He stands at the doorway and rubs the back of his neck awkwardly. 'They cut you. Nobody told me they were going to cut you. I never expected them to do that!'

My heart feels like it will burst with the love I feel for this man. 'Come here, you big oaf, and meet your son,' I say gruffly.

He comes forward eagerly.

'Sit down,' I say and when he does I put Sergei into his large hands. It is a moment I will remember forever. Our baby fits into his cupped hands. His face softens as he looks at the magic we have created together.

'He's so small. Is this normal?' he asks worriedly.

'Excuse me. Try pushing him out of your cock then tell me he's small,' I retort.

He flushes a deep red.

Immediately my heart goes out to him. He is so Russian when it comes to pregnancies and babies. Utterly lost and baffled. 'He is eight pounds and two ounces. That's a good size,' I tell him reassuringly.

Sergei moves his head and yawns a gummy, healthy yawn. Awwww my son just yawned.

'Did you see that? He yawned,' Noah says excitedly.

We look at each other,both of us so deeply in love with the little person we have created we have become foolish with it.

He takes a deep breath. 'I'm sorry I ... er ... fainted.'

I laugh. 'Yes, how did that happen anyway?'

He shakes his head. 'I don't know. I can look at my own blood, and the blood of other men, but I can't fucking see you spill blood. It just made my head spin, and before I knew it I was gone.'

'Oh, Noah.'

He comes forward and kisses me gently. 'You were just amazing. I'm so proud of you. I just can't believe I missed it all.'

'Never mind next time—'

He frowns. 'Next time? You want to go through this again?' he asks incredulously.

'Of course. Sergei needs brothers and sisters. I don't want him to be an only child like me.'

'No,' he says decisively. 'I think you suffered enough. I don't think we will have any more kids. We can adopt. There are so many kids that need a good home.'

'No way. We've having at least four kids, maybe five, and if you want we can adopt a couple too, but the next time I go into labor you can stay close to my head.'

'We'll have to talk about this,' he says darkly.

There is a knock on the door and Baba comes in holding a covered bowl of food. She frowns. 'Why is that baby not swaddled?' she demands immediately. 'First you break custom by going out and buying clothes and toys for the child before it is born now you don't want to swaddle the baby,' she tuts with displeasure.

I giggle. 'Mama didn't swaddle me and I turned out okay, didn't I?'

'That remains to be seen,' she says, pretending to be sour but beaming with joy.

'Where's Mama anyway?' I ask.

'She's coming. She met the doctor and decided to have a word with him.'

At that moment my mother comes into the room.

'Oh darling, well done.' She rushes to Noah's side and peers at the baby.

'Oh, my goodness me. he's so beautiful.'

'Yes, he is the most beautiful boy in the whole world.'

Epilogue

Noah Abramovich
Half A Century Later

https://www.youtube.com/watch?v=iQo
p_qs4xV4
How Long Will I love You?

I press the soil around the tomato seedling, water it, and sit back on my haunches. It's mid-morning and the Sicilian sun is already hot on my back. I pull the cowboy hat low on my brow and stand. Straightening my aching back I start walking back towards house. Tasha should be home soon. Ivan, our second son, came over to take her to the market to buy crabs for lunch.

I pass by the olive grove where all Tasha's dogs are buried. Every single one and there have been many. Even Sergei. She had his body exhumed and brought it here to be buried close to her.

As I walk I see our daughter, Tatiana, who should be in her own home today, running towards me, and I immediately freeze. Then I start running towards her too. We meet near the wooden swing that Tasha and I sit on to watch the sunset while we eat and drink vodka.

'What's the matter?' I ask, catching her by her forearms. Her eyes are red. She has been crying.

'It's Mama,' she pants breathless.

It feels as if my heart stops with fear.

'What has happened?' I demand.

'Ivan has had to take her to the hospital. She slipped on a wet patch in the market and fell.' Her eyes fill with tears. 'Oh Papa, Ivan had to carry her because she couldn't walk. He's been trying to call you, Papa, but no one answered the phone.'

'I was working on the land.' I pull her along with me. 'Come on, let's get to the hospital now.'

'Your hands, papa.'

I look at my hands. They are streaked with soil. I wash my hands in the kitchen then we get into her car and she drives us. The hospital is nearly forty minutes away. I try to call Ivan repeatedly, but his phone is shut off.

'They probably don't allow phones at the hospital,' Tatiana says.

'Can't you drive faster?' I ask my daughter.

'I'm going as fast as I can, Daddy.'

Inside I am cold. I start praying. *Please, don't let her be in pain. Give me that pain. I can bear it better than her.*

In thirty minutes we reach the hospital and rush in. We ask at reception and they point us to where Ivan and Tasha are. We rush to the emergency ward and I see her lying on a gurney. She looks so small and vulnerable. I rush to her and she smiles at me through the pain.

'My life, my life,' I whisper.

'It's only a sprain, but I was trying to persuade them to give me some morphine anyway,' she says with a grin.

Tears of relief come to my eyes. Oh, God! I cannot even begin to imagine my life without my Tasha. She used to tease me by calling me the strong and silent type. I don't mean to be quiet, but when I speak she stops talking, and my ears ache for the sound of her voice.

'I thought your leg was broken. Tatiana said Ivan had to carry you.' I say.

'You know what Ivan is like. He's worse than you. I could have easily walked, but of course, he insisted on carrying me. It was embarrassing, actually.' She scrunches up her nose. 'People probably thought I was too old to walk on my own or something.'

I touch her face, running my fingertips on her cheeks. 'You are the only seventy-year old woman I know without any wrinkles.'

'Have you been looking at a whole pile of seventy-year old women again?' she asks with a laugh.

'I haven't looked at another woman since the day you sneaked into my office in your sexy pink cardigan.'

'Oh, you old flatterer, you.' She laughs and it makes my heart beat slower. *She's fine. She's fine.*

'It's the truth. You were the most beautiful woman I ever saw and you still are.'

She smiles. 'And you Noah Abramovich are the most good-looking fucker I ever saw.'

'Are you being hot on purpose?'

She winks. 'What do you think?

'We'll see if you're so cocky once I get you home, you saucy wench.'

'Will someone wrap my damn ankle up quickly so I can get the hell home, she says grumpily, and then goes and spoils the effect by laughing that beautiful laugh of hers again.

The End

FUN BONUS

(A Day In The Life Of Crystal Jake)

https://www.youtube.com/watch?v=7oK
PYe53h78
You're The One I Want

My sleep is disturbed by something tickling my ear. I open my eyes and automatically turn towards Lily. She is fast asleep. In fact, the tickling is coming from the other side. I turn my face. In the gloom of my bedroom, my daughter's little face floats next to my head. I stretch my eyes open. 'What?'

She puts her finger to her lips. 'Shhhh.'

I nod.

She leans forwards and cupping her hands around my ears whispers, 'Daddy, let's make pancakes for Mummy.'

'What time is it?' I whisper back.

'Time to wake up.'

Silly me. Of course, what else would it be? The alarm o'clock says six o'clock.

'Where are your brothers?'

'Sleeping,' she dismisses scornfully.

I slip on a pair of sweat pants and we tiptoe out of the room as stealthy as cat burglars. We go down the stairs and our long-suffering dog wakes up, gives a huge stretch and, wagging his tail, follows us. The cat opens an eye, then goes right back to sleep. We go into the kitchen, lit by the early morning summer sun shining brightly through the windows. I lift Liliana up and put her on the island top. I inhale the top of her head. My daughter smells like a slice of heaven in the mornings.

'Daddy, can we make pancakes like how you and Mummy make them?'

'What do you mean?'

'We dance and hug while we make them.' She swirls her fingers.

I laugh. 'Oh. That. Sure. We can dance like that while we make them.'

'Put on a song for us, then.'

'Which one?'

'The thousand years one. The one with the words, I've loved you for a thousand years, and I'll love you for another thousand.' It is endearing the way she drags out the word thousand.

I smile at her. 'I can't dance to that with you. That's Mummy and Daddy's song. I promised Mummy that will be our special song.'

Her face becomes thoughtful. 'But what about me? We don't have a special song.'

'How about you pick a song and that'll be our song. I won't dance to it with anyone else.'

'Yesssss,' she cries, her eyes filling up with excitement. Then she stops and looks at me slyly. 'You won't even dance with Mummy?'

'Not even Mummy,' I confirm. One day my daughter is going to make some poor fool's life hell on earth.

She puts her hands on her hips. 'What if Mummy asks you to?'

'I'll say no,' I tell her firmly.

Her eyes narrow to accusing slits. She usually reserves this expression for her brothers and cousins. 'But you never say no to Mummy.'

'Yes, I do.'

'No, you don't.'

'Yes, I do.'

'When have you said no?' she demands, with her little chin pushed out.

I rub my face and consider the question. Hmmm. Out of the mouth of babes. My daughter could have a point. I can't remember the last time I said no to Lily.

I grin suddenly. 'Sometimes Mummy says, "You stink. Go have a bath." And I say, "no."'

She dissolves into giggles. 'You're lying, Daddy.'

'Fine, how about the next time Mummy asks me to do something I'll say no?'

'Okay,' she agrees with the sweet naivety and innocence of children.

'Pick a song then.'

She thinks. 'I don't know Daddy. There are too many.'

'Well, do you want something happy, sweet, or funny?'

'I want something happy,' she says immediately and decisively.

'Let me see if I can find something that's perfect for us,' I say going over to the music deck. She trails behind me. I see that my mother must been around because Olivia Newton John's greatest hits is at the top of the selection. I look at my daughter and suddenly I know the perfect father and daughter routine for us.

'Oh Liliana, I think I found us the best song ever. Come on, I'll show you. I pull up You Tube and look for that old favorite, *You're the One That I Want* performed by Olivia Newton John and John Travolta. I put it on full screen, switch it on, and let her watch. She seems transfixed.

When it is finished, I pause it. 'Like it?'

She nods vigorously.

'Is it good enough for us?'

'Yup.'

'Want to see it again?'

'Yup.'

We watch it two more times before I stop it and say, 'Think we can do the same?'

She grins. 'I can. My part's easy-peasy,' she says confidently.

'Good.'

'Wait for me I'll be back,' she says, and races off upstairs.

I go into the kitchen and take out the ingredients and utensils for making pancakes. She comes into the kitchen wearing her sparkly red shoes and carrying one of my shirts.

'You need a shirt to twirl.'

'Thank you,' I say, taking the shirt from her and putting it on.

I locate the track on iTunes and turn towards her. 'Ready?' I ask.

'Yes.'

The kitchen fills with music and I start making my moves ala Travolta while she watches and waits for her turn to join in. I know that we are on to a winner by the way she is nodding her head and shaking her little hips to the music the way Olivia did.

'It's electrifying,' I mime, and shaking my body as if I have been electrocuted, I fall to the ground. Liliana twists the cigarette she has been pretending to smoke under the heel of her sparkly shoes and as I start to rise up, puts her tiny foot on my chest, and pushes me back down.

Then she struts away like a real pro and I start chasing after her. Instead of a flight of stairs that Olivia went up, Liliana starts climbing up the steps into her brother's cot while I pretend to writhe at the bottom of it. When she starts beckoning me with her little finger, I begin to wish I had recorded this. Lily so needs to see this. She is so incredibly cute. I don't know that she'll be able to repeat this performance exactly like this when we do it again. Then we do that thing they do in the Shake Shack. Then both hands on the front of the hips and small steps forward. And we end with her legs wrapped around my waist.

'Oo Oo Oo you're the one that I need,' both of us sing.

'You were brilliant,' I tell her. And I really mean it. My daughter is a born star.

'Shall we do it again?'

'What about the pancakes?'

'Smile both of you,' Lily says from the doorway. She is holding her video camera in her hand.

'Mummy, you recorded us!'

'I did.'

'Let me see. Let me see.'

Lily comes forward and the three of us watch the performance. I'm not bad, but Liliana is amazing.

I put Liliana on the countertop and she immediately reaches for the camera.

'You've left your big old fingerprints on the screen, Missie. Pass me a tissue, please, Jake,' Lily asks.

I reach for it and my daughter clears her throat noisily.

I turn to look at her and she raises her eyebrows in the most adorable way.

I turn to Lily. 'No.'

My daughter nods with approval and Lily looks at me with surprise. 'Darling, it's right next to you.'

'No. Get it yourself.'

My daughter grins, my wife sighs elaborately. 'What are both of you up to now?'

'Nothing,' Liliana says innocently.

'Fine, I'll get it myself.'

'Don't worry Mummy. 'I'll get the tissue for you,' Liliana says.

Oh, the little rat!

Completely avoiding my eyes, she gives her mother the tissue.

'Go wake your brothers up, and we'll feed the birds together,' Lily says.

'Okay,' Liliana agrees happily and runs away.

'So what was that all about?' Lily asks, her eyebrows arched.

'Well, our daughter noticed that I never say no to you and I kinda said I'd say no to the next thing you asked.'

She gasps. 'That cheeky, troublemaking little monkey.'

'I'd go with rat.'

'I don't know why she's like that. It not from my side of the family. I was a goody two shoes.'

I put my hands up. 'Don't look at me. I was an angel.'

A mischievous look comes into her eyes. 'What if the first thing I asked you had been, "Jake, will you fuck me?"'

'Then Liliana will have to resign herself to a father who doesn't keep his word, or find herself a different father.'

She shakes her head. 'I can't believe that girl.'

I put my arms around her waist and lift her up onto the counter. 'And I can't believe how fabulously sexy you looked last night.'

'Um ... I think you showed me last night.'

I grab her ass and my cock swells. 'God, I want to show you again, right now.'

She looks up at me. 'The kids will be down soon, and anyway, don't you have to get to work soon?'

'Yeah, I do, but don't forget you're down for a long session tonight. I'm packing the kids off to Shane. They're staying there overnight.'

She grins. 'A whole night? You're sure you're up to it?'

'That there, young lady. That just earned you a spanking.'

'Let's do that thing we never do when the kids are around,' she whispers.

I become hard as a rock.

Of course, at that moment our children come running into the room. Deliciously small and chubby and full of energy. Morning greetings and sloppy kisses are given and received.

'What about the pancakes, Daddy?'

'Nah, it's too late for those. We'll do them tomorrow.'

Then I kiss Lily goodbye and stand at the window drinking my coffee and watching them go out into the large field behind the house, each one carrying a little bucket of birdfeed, bread crumbs and crushed dog biscuits.

They are my life.

Liliana runs out ahead with the boys running behind her and Lily lagging behind. I watch them throw the food on to the large feeding platform. There are already a few birds waiting, but suddenly a whole crowd of crows descends on them. There must be at least fifty. It is a magnificent sight.

After they have fed the birds they will go to see the horses, so I go upstairs and get into the shower. When I come out Lily and the kids are still not back, but staff have started arriving. I dress quickly and leave the house.

The roads are fairly clear and I get into work pretty quickly. I pick up a paper at receptionist, get into the lift, and hit the button for my floor. When the doors open I stroll into to my secretary, Eliza's, office. She looks at me strangely.

'Your brother is here.'

'Dom or Shane?'

She widens her eyes. 'Neither?'

I stare at her. 'What?'

'He says he's your brother.'

I look at her with a bemused expression. Is she serious?

'His name is Tyson Eden.'

'Where is he now?'

'In your office.'

'You let him go into my office? A complete stranger?'

She nods, a funny expression on her face. 'Yeah.'

What the fuck is going on? I stride to my door, open it and come to a dead stop. No wonder Eliza let him decide where he should wait. The cocky bastard is sitting in my chair with his ankles crossed and up on my table. He is wearing a string vest and his chest and arms are tattooed. His face ... it's like looking into the fucking mirror.

Dad, you old dog, you!

Coming soon to a kindle near you ... Tyson Eden

Coming next... Jack Irish

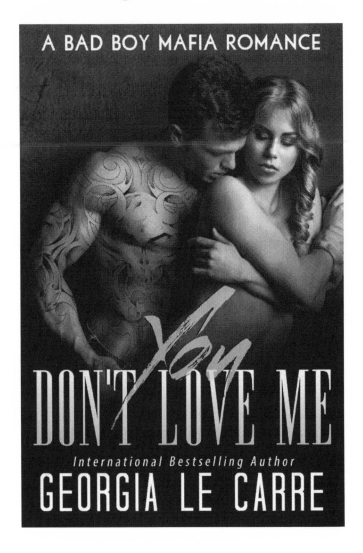

A BAD BOY MAFIA ROMANCE

You

DON'T LOVE ME

International Bestselling Author

GEORGIA LE CARRE

Thank you for reading everybody!

Please click on this link to receive news of my latest releases and giveaways.
http://bit.ly/1oe9WdE

and remember

I **LOVE** hearing from readers so by all means come and say hello here:

https://www.facebook.com/georgia.lecar
re

43662902R00210

Made in the USA
Middletown, DE
27 April 2019